Copyright © 2022 by Samantha Barrett
All rights reserved.
No part of this book may be reproduced in any form or by any electronic or
mechanical means, including information storage and retrieval systems, without
written permission from the author, except for the use of brief quotations in a
book review.

This is a work of fiction. Names, characters, businesses, places, events and
incidents are either the products of the author's imagination or used in a
fictitious manner. Any similarities to real people, places, or events are entirely
coincidental.

All Rights reserved. No part of this publication may be reproduced, stored in a
retrieval system, or transmitted in any form or by any means, electronic,
mechanical, recording or otherwise, without the prior written permission of the
copyright holder.

"Lake William" is dedicated to my cousin.
May you rest easy, and soar high.
Wiremu "William" Vincent Kahui

Chapter One

I wake in the woods again, wearing the same white summer dress I always am. I didn't need to call out—I knew he would be here. He always is. Glancing over my shoulder, I lock eyes with him. I know it's a dream, but God, it feels so real. The raw sexual attraction between us in the air is almost like a fuse to a bomb. The closer we get to each other, the closer we are to detonating.

"Hello, love." His voice is pure sin and virulent masculine sexiness.

"Hi." I can hear the lust in my own voice, making it husky and soft.

He looks at me like I am his last meal. It sends shivers down my spine and liquid pooling between my thighs.

"Come here, love." I saunter over to him, admiring his beauty. He towers over me at six foot three. He wears jeans that hang low on his hips, showcasing that beautiful V. He's sans shirt, as always. My eyes travel to his face, his beautiful full lips turned up at the corners in a smirk. Those eyes are so captivating and the deepest violet in color. Yeah, I know no one has violet-colored eyes, but this is my dream, and I'll have what I want. His jet black hair is slicked back, like he has just run his hand through it.

I stand in front of my dream man, so close I can feel the heat radiating off his body. He pulls me flush against his chest, and I gasp at the contact. The heat from his body is making me burn, in the most delicious way.

"You're so beautiful, love. I could never get enough of you." My dream man always knows the right things to say. Before I can respond, he stops my reply with a kiss of such force that it steals my breath. I wrap my arms around his neck, and he slides his hands down my thighs and lifts me off the ground. Instinctively, I wind my legs around his waist. We never break our kiss. He walks us a few steps forward and lowers me to the grass.

"I can smell how wet you are for me," he whispers against my lips.

I need him inside me now. I need his mouth on mine like I need my next breath. He pulls the thin straps of my dress down each arm, exposing my breasts. I don't have small boobs, but they aren't large either. What is it they say? "More than a handful is waste." He moves his head down to my breast and starts to suck hard, just the way I like it. I sigh in pleasure as he continues to suck and bite my nipples. His right hand slides my dress up to expose my lower half—I never wear panties in my dreams. He slides his hand between my soaking wet folds, and as soon as his fingers graze my enlarged nub, I scream out. I am so close to coming already, and he knows it. He withdraws his hand and mouth from my body and leans back, peering down at me with a smirk. He knows what he is doing to me and he loves every second of it.

I lean forward and unbutton his jeans, pulling them down so I can expose his cock. When it springs free, I smile. It always takes my breath away. He is so large that his hard length nearly hits his navel. I start to stroke him roughly, and he hisses through clenched teeth.

He wiggles out of his jeans then pushes me back down so I'm

lying flat on my back, his hard body hovering over mine. The heat of his kiss makes more liquid gather between my legs. I am so fucking wet for him. He positions himself between my legs, then slams into me. I swear I can feel him hitting the back of my womb, and the combination of pleasure and the slight sting of pain forces a moan from me.

"Scream for me, love," he whispers in my ear, while driving into me. I can feel how close I am already, a moment later he has me screaming out.

"I'm coming, Nico! God, don't fucking stop," I scream, clawing at his back like a possessed woman.

"Come on my cock, love. I love feeling your pussy clench my dick." His words are my undoing, and I come almost violently while screaming his name to the heavens. But he isn't done with me yet, and he wrings another orgasm from me before he finds his own release. Once he's spent, he collapses on top of me, both of us panting like we have just run a marathon. It feels like we have. Once my breathing is under control, I open my eyes to look at Nico.

"I know this is all a dream, but God I wish you were real." As soon as the words leave my mouth, it all goes dark.

I woke panting and out of breath, my hair sticking to my forehead and cheek. My steamy dreams always left me this way, but I wouldn't change it for the world. In my dreams I was strong, confident, and sexy—and adored by my men. I was none of those things in real life: I always second-guessed my decisions, and my long hair was plain Jane brown. I had strange eyes that seemed to unnerve people. They were a bright shade of green, and there was a ring of yellow around my pupils. I was not adored by anyone in real life. My mother beat me throughout my childhood, and my father left with my twin sister just after we turned five.

My mother would tell me that she was preparing me for when "the others" would come. I never knew what that meant, and if I tried to ask, she would simply say I needed to toughen up. That was always her excuse for beating me and locking me in my room for days on end. "A weak bitch can't lead anyone," she'd yell when I begged her to let me out. "You will die after a day, if you don't suck it up." She told me there come a time when I would be caged, and I needed to learn how to cope.

Shaking myself from my inner thoughts, I peeled the covers

off my sweat-laden body and went to grab some clothes from my bag so I could have a quick shower. I had stopped at a hotel the night before, too tired to drive the full distance to Stevie's house.

I still had a long drive ahead of me to reach my sister, and we still had a lot to get ready in the two days before we left on our big trip to Alaska. My life was finally my own and not ruled by my mother, and I was going to enjoy every moment of it, with my sister by my side.

I was almost bouncing in my seat with excitement as I arrived at my sister's house. There were two cars in the driveway; I knew one was Stevie's beat-up old Mini, but I had no idea who owned the other.

As I got out of my truck, I heard the front door swing open. My sister came running out to greet me. She looked as beautiful, as always. She was the better-looking twin, with long brown hair and hazel eyes—with no weird yellow ring around her pupils. She had a slim figure with curves in all the right places, and even in a plain white V-neck shirt and a pair of worn-out jeans with tears in the legs, she still looked like a Victoria's Secret model.

"Sissy!" she screeched as she pulled me in for a bone-crushing hug.

"Hey, Stevie," I murmured, hugging her back.

"How was your drive? You must be tired. Come on, let's get your bags and get inside. I'm freezing my balls off." I couldn't help but laugh at my sister, who continued her chatter as we pulled my two bags from the trunk. She never had a filter— not that I was any different. My mouth always got me in trouble with my mom, but I just couldn't help it. I am who I am, I guess.

"So, do you want to tell me who that car belongs to? Or do I have to guess?" I asked. She always had boys falling all over her, so it wouldn't surprise me if it belonged to some guy she knew.

"Oh, you will just have to wait and see when you get inside. It's a surprise! I'm sure you'll love it," she said with a wink.

Now I was on guard. My sister was always one for the dramatics. You never knew what to expect when she said she had a surprise for you. I just hoped it was nothing like the surprise she sent me for my sixteenth birthday. I have never hated a gift more. She had one of our cousins—Chase—show up at my high school and bring me flowers and chocolates and act like he was my new boyfriend! She did this because my ex had recently dumped me in front of the whole football team. They all laughed their ugly asses off. Needless to say, don't ever tell Stevie when a guy dumps you.

As soon as we passed the threshold of the front door, I was grabbed from behind lifted off my feet.

"Put me down!" I yelled, trying to wriggle around and see who the hell had grabbed me.

Once on my feet, I swung around to see my cousin Chase hunched over, laughing his ass off. He looked up with those sky blue eyes, and I couldn't help the grin that tugged at my lips. Once he stood to his full height, he was over six feet tall.

"I can't believe you still scream like a girl," he said, still chuckling.

"That's because I am a girl, you jackass," I huffed.

"Now, now, you two—cut it out. You know you love him still, Ry, even if you did fake break up with him in eleventh grade," Stevie said, grinning like a fool.

Chase gasped. "Oh my God! Yes! Stevie, you still owe me for that. Ryan nearly punched me in the face that day for telling her friends I was her boyfriend."

I narrowed my eyes. "I hate you both."

Just as I turned away from their giggling nonsense, I was grabbed again and let out another screech, sending Chase and Stevie into howls of laughter once more.

"Holy shit, she sounds like a cat that got its tail stepped on," Chase said between guffaws.

Once I was put back on my feet for the second time that day, I looked up to see my other cousin—Chase's older brother, Alex.

"Alex!" I pulled him in for a hug. I hadn't seen Alex in years. Chase and Alex were my uncle's sons, from my dad's side. I was never allowed to visit them, and Mom had told me that my uncle hated me because I lived with her. I found out after Mom went missing that my uncle didn't hate me—it was just Mom trying to turn me against Dad's side of the family.

"Hey, squirt, how are you? It's been way too long. I see you finally grew into your big head," Alex joked.

I smiled sweetly at him. "Aww, it must run in the family. You finally grew into your ears." Looking at the beautiful man that now stood in front of me, it was hard to believe he was the same kid who was called Dumbo on the playground. He still had his coal black hair and baby blue eyes, though. He was a bit taller than Chase, but not by much, with a strong jaw line and high, defined cheekbones. He could have been a model—heck, maybe he was. I didn't know very much about these boys anymore.

In spite of Chase's sandy blond hair, the brothers looked

very much alike. They also looked like they spent every spare minute they had at the gym.

"All right, enough of the pleasantries, family. Ryan's had a long drive, and I am sure she would love to take a shower and rest before dinner." *Bless you, Stevie, for reading my mind.*

"I would really love a shower. I feel icky after the long drive." Chase and Alex started giggling like schoolgirls. I pinned them both with a glare.

"And what the hell is so funny now, you two goons?" I snapped.

"Well, for one, no one outside of first grade says icky," Chase said with a snort, trying to cover his laughter.

"Shut up. Lots of people say icky," I argued.

"Oh yeah, like who, squirt?" Alex was grinning at me now.

"Well, I can't think of anyone right this second, but..." I was cut off as all three of them started laughing their asses off at my expense.

"Okay, okay. Chase, you start getting the meat on the grill. Alex you can make us all some drinks while I take Ryan up to her room. Once you're done with the drinks, Alex, can you bring Ryan's bags up?" Stevie was like an army general barking out orders to everyone.

Both the boys gave a nod and went about their tasks. On the way up the stairs, I paused to look at the many photos that lined the wall, almost all of them of Stevie, from her first day of school to her graduation, and photos of her on her birthday—well, our birthday. The one that got my attention had Stevie, Dad, and me in it. We must have been about 4 years old, and one of us was perched on each of his knees and smiling. I wished I could have gone with my Dad and Stevie when they left, but my mom wouldn't let both of us go. Truth be told, she only wanted to keep one of us so Dad had to pay her child support.

Stevie noticed I had stopped following her up the stairs, and she came back down and wrapped an arm around my shoulders. She knew it was hard for me to see the photos. She had the happy childhood and a loving parent. I had neither.

"He never stopped loving you, and he talked about you all the time."

"Then why did he never fight for me? He never came back *once* after you left, Stevie, He left me with her! I would have given my firstborn child to have been with you and Dad. I never had a choice." I knew she wouldn't have let me go with them, no matter what Dad said, but it still hurt to have been virtually abandoned.

My sister looked at me with such pity in her eyes, but I didn't want her pity or anyone else's. I had no intention of letting my mother's abuse define me. I am not a victim; I am a survivor.

"I don't know, Ryan. For years I asked him if you could come for holidays or if I could go visit you and Mom. He always said no to me visiting you. He rang Mom a few times to ask if you could come here. He told her it wasn't healthy to keep us apart. She would always tell him he could see you again when he got over himself and came back to her."

There wasn't much to say after that, so I just sighed and started my trek up the stairs. Once at the top, she opened the second door on the right. The room was beautiful, with painted pink walls and a queen-sized bed in the middle of the room. There was a unicorn plushie perched on the bed, even. I used to love unicorns. There was a single dresser on the far wall with little snow globes on top. I made my way over to inspect them further, only to be distracted by a note on the side table by the bed that was addressed to me. I raised a brow at Stevie in question.

"The letter is from Dad. He wrote it to you the week he passed. It was like he almost knew what was coming. Dad always said one day you would come back here. He never gave up hope, Ry. He wanted his girls back together. This was supposed to be your room."

I looked to my sister, my mouth hanging open. Her words set an ache in my heart. I had dreamed of a room like this when I was little, instead of the dirty mattress on the floor with no sheets. Mom never spent money on things that weren't an absolute necessity. She always told me I should be grateful it wasn't the floor.

"If he wanted me to come back here so bad, why didn't he open the front door and let me see you when I came here, Stevie? I don't understand any of this." I was trying so hard to hold back the tears. My sister looked at me with utter heartbreak in her eyes, and I forced myself to swallow down the pain. I couldn't take that look from her.

"Don't worry, Stevie. I just want to grab a shower and relax. It's supposed to be a happy time. We're finally together again, and no one is here to tear us apart this time. We'll deal with all this other crap later."

She smiled, but it didn't reach her eyes. She simply took my hand in hers and squeezed it tight once before leaving me in my pink room with my unicorn and my grief.

After having a long, hot shower, some of the stress from my drive and the memories of my childhood start to ease. I was thankful for that; I didn't want to spoil this time with my sister and cousins by living in the past. While brushing out my hair and staring at myself in the mirror, I thought about how different mine and Stevie's personalities are. She has such a carefree spirit, and I always worry and over-think things. She has so much confidence and could hold her own in a room full of beautiful people, where-as I would sit in a corner, hoping no one would notice I was even there.

I leave the bathroom quickly and change into my favorite pair of jeans, which had tears in the knees. I grab the first shirt I can find; it's a Harley Quinn and Joker printed T-shirt. What can I say? I loved their crazy, unorthodox love. It made me want to find someone who would love all *my* craziness. I loved how they both changed to fit together as one. I wanted someone to love me the way the Joker loves Harley—but with less homicide.

As I started to descend the stairs, I could hear raised voices. I wasn't planning on listening to their conversation, but when I heard my name, I couldn't help it. I crouched on the stairs and listened intently.

"What do you mean, Ryan doesn't know?" Alex snapped.

"Keep your voice down, Alex, I haven't had a chance to tell her, and Dad never got around to it. He thought he had more time." I could hear the hurt in Stevie's voice when she mentioned our dad.

Our father died suddenly, three months after Stevie and I turned eighteen. I did not attend his funeral, as I thought he wouldn't want me there. I would learn later that was not the case at all, and I would forever regret not attending and saying goodbye to my dad.

"She has to be told who she really is and what she is capable of, before she hurts herself or someone else, Stevie." Chase sounded annoyed at Stevie's reluctance.

"I plan on telling her when the time is right. She has been through a lot, and just being here, in this house, is hard for her. She didn't grow up like us, with a loving parent. She has built all these walls up around herself, and I don't want to drop this on her and risk her having a breakdown." Wow, clearly it was something big if she thought I would have a breakdown.

I couldn't quite understand what this big secret was that they were keeping from me. I mean, I know we didn't all grow up together, but we always found ways to talk on the phone. When they came to visit, I would sneak out after Mom fell asleep or passed out. She only caught me sneaking out once, and let me tell you, I couldn't sit for a week afterwards. She whipped me like a dog, splitting the skin on my rear open. I screamed so loud I thought the neighbors would call the cops. Hell, I wanted them to call them. After getting whipped twelve times, I was locked in my room for the next two days, with no food or water, just my mattress and a bucket in the corner.

"You need to tell her soon, Stevie, or Chase and I will. She has a right to know, for God's sake. She could have protected herself from your mom, if you or your dad had just told her," Alex whisper-shouted. This was getting more interesting by the minute.

"Don't you fucking think we wanted to, Alex? We tried to tell her so many times. We went to their house *six times* and got turned away by my so-called mother. She said if we ever came back, she would out us to the humans! What do you think we should have done? Kept going back? Risk being exposed to the world? That drunken, drugged-up bitch would have sung like a bird, and you know it!" Stevie had so much hate in her voice when she mentioned our mother.

I was done listening to their conversation *about me*, which was happening *without* me, my fury building as I heard about things for the first time. Unfortunately, as I turned to go back upstairs, my foot caught on the stair tread, and I fell, letting out an involuntary shriek as I bounced and rolled. I was waiting for the last bang, when I knew I would connect with the tile floor, but suddenly I stopped. When I opened my eyes, I saw my sister and cousins in the kitchen doorway, mouths hanging open and eyes wide. I looked down and realized my body was levitating a few inches off the floor and emanating a blue light. I let out another scream, and my body dropped the remainder of the way to the ground with a thud. Within seconds, the others were on either side of me, barking questions.

"Are you ok, Ry?"

"How did you do that?"

"Are you hurt anywhere?"

I couldn't think, let alone answer questions. I lay there for a few moments, mind whirling and body groaning, before finally answering.

"I'm fine, and no, I'm not hurt. I have no idea what the hell that was. I'm a bit creeped out by it, to be honest."

I caught a glimpse of pride in my sister's eyes before she quickly masked it. Why would she look at me like that? I have never levitated before, but I have seen the blue light a couple of times. I've never told anybody about it, because first of all, who would believe me, and second, I didn't quite believe it myself.

"Well, it was cool, but let's not dwell on it. Dinner is nearly ready, so come on, up you go, Sissy." Stevie was already pulling me up before she finished speaking.

Chase and Alex both exchanged looks I couldn't quite read. I thanked them and followed them into the kitchen. It was slightly dated, with vintage cabinets lining the walls, but there was a massive, stainless steel gas stove. Alex and Chase were both sitting at the breakfast bar on two of the four bar stools. Stevie was on the other side of the bar, assembling a salad. I sat next to the boys, still reeling at what the hell had just happened, when Alex nudged me.

"What?" I asked

"Didn't you hear what Chase said?" Truth be told, I hadn't heard a word.

"Ummm...No, sorry, can you please say it again, Chase? I was off with the fairies there for a second." I forced a smile with my words, so they wouldn't worry about where my head was at.

"Totally understandable, but I was just wondering how your last day of school went, and did you hear anything more from the cops?" He looked like he was scared to ask the last part. I knew all of them were wondering the same thing, so I thought I may as well get it out of the way now and just be open and honest with them about Mom's disappearance.

"I haven't heard anything from the detective who was the lead on Mom's case. They said there isn't much more that they could do, as she did leave a note, and I'm an adult. To them, she willingly left and that's not a crime."

"What note? You never said she left a note." Stevie looked

annoyed, and I winced. The reason I never told her was because the contents of the note were spiteful.

"I never told you about the note because what she wrote was not nice, Stevie. She said a lot of stupid shit in it. None of which is true, so to save you the hurt, I never said anything. I'm sorry for keeping it from you."

"I know you just want to protect me, Ry, as I do you, but you don't have to. I'm a big girl. Can you please just tell me what the note said?"

"She said that now that Dad is dead, she doesn't get paid for me, and wasn't going to stick around to raise the bastards that still to this day are mistakes that should never have happened. Also, she wished she had left me years ago."

The words in the note hurt more than what I wanted them to. Part of me always wanted my mom to love me. I guess you always want the love of your parents, no matter what they do to you. She was all I had. I knew she had a drug and alcohol problem, and I tried to blame her abuse and neglect on that, but I knew deep down that it wasn't.

"Damn," Alex and Chase both hissed in unison.

"I don't really know what to say to that, to be honest. I knew she had issues with having us young, but I never thought she would hate us like she obviously did. I mean, we never fucking asked to be born." I knew where Stevie was coming from—I felt the same way. "She should have kept her fucking legs shut if she didn't want us. I am glad to be here, though." She said the last part with a cheeky smile and a squeeze of my shoulder.

"She has a lot of demons she needs to work out on her own. I think I'm just glad that she didn't try to kill me before she left," I said with a nervous laugh, which betrayed the bitter truth of my admission.

"Don't say shit like that! It's not funny, Ryan" Alex scolded with a stern look.

"I'm sorry. I didn't mean it; it's just it was hard to live with her. She used to say she would end me before she let me go. I'm sorry. I didn't mean to bring the mood down. Can we change the subject and talk about something else, like what you've been doing?"

"Okay, fine. We'll let it go *for now*. We still have to get shit ready for our trip. I'm so excited! I cannot wait to get the hell out of this town and go on a trip with my three favorite people. Oh, that's right, Ryan! I forgot to tell you that part of the surprise is that Alex and Chase are going to be coming with us." My sister was just full of surprises today, wasn't she? But I was super excited that my cousins would be taking this trip with us.

"Well, that's just awesome. I'm so glad you two are coming with us. It wouldn't be as much fun without you both," I said, nudging Chase.

"I'm as keen as a jelly bean to go on this trip. Alex and I have been looking forward to this for months now, and I'm glad we don't have to keep it a secret anymore." Chase said all this while looking my sister directly in the eye, almost as if hinting that now would be a good time for the big reveal. I have to admit, I am dying to know what Stevie is hiding from me.

"I second you there, my brother," Alex said while grinning at me and waggling his brows.

"We need to get the house in order before we go, so let's have some dinner and then get packing and sorting this house out." My sister always loved to boss everyone around. We did as she asked; it was easier than having to deal with the bitch fit she would throw if we didn't.

Chapter Four

The two days flew by as we packed, cleaned, and locked the house up. My aunt (Alex & Chase's mom) would be checking on Stevie's house while we were away. It was really nice of her to do that, as we would be away for three months. I couldn't freaking wait to finally ride on a plane and have adventures with my sister and cousins, something that had been impossible until now.

I hadn't had any of my dreams since arriving at Stevie's; I was really starting to miss my dream guys. I know it sounds silly, but Nico and Kai made me feel so alive. Oh yeah, I forgot to mention, Nico wasn't my only dream sex god. I had another god-like man in my dreams. His name is Kai, and he is just as yummy as Nico. I had been trying to dream of each of them for the past two nights, but it was like they weren't at home, which had never happened before. I was a little worried, to be honest.

Stevie and I were dragging our bags down the stairs, when we heard Chase yell out.

"Yo! Cab's here! Move your asses, ladies; we need to go."

Stevie and I glanced at each other, grinning in anticipation. We hurried the rest of the way down the stairs to the front door.

I followed Alex out with my suitcase trailing behind me, and Stevie stopped just outside the door. I turned to see her holding her hand over the door handle whispering something, and then I saw her hand glow. I gasped and almost tripped on the path by the taxi. I thought I was the only weird one—a freak, as my mom used to say. Stevie began to walk toward me with her bags in tow, eyebrows raised as she saw my expression.

"Ry, why do you look so shocked?" Stevie asked.

"Your hand! I saw what you did. I saw your hand glow," I screeched.

Stevie shared a look with the boys before bringing her eyes back to me.

"I don't know what you're talking about. You did bump your head the other night, so you could be seeing things. Now hurry, before we miss our flight."

Stevie continued on to the cab like nothing had happened, but I know what I saw. There was no way I had imagined that. The strangest part was that her hand had glowed like mine had done a few times when my emotions got out of control, my glow was blue, but Stevie's was purple. This obviously wasn't the time to get into all that, though, so I shook it off and decided to corner my sister on the long plane ride.

We arrived at the airport twenty minutes later. Once all the bags were out and the driver was paid, we all made our way into the airport to check our bags and go through security.

. . .

Once seated on the plane, I finally started to relax. I was actually going on my first-ever plane ride! My first trip abroad – I was beyond excited to be leaving New Zealand.

Once the plane took off, everyone started to get comfortable. We had a long flight ahead of us: sixteen hours to Los Angeles and a further seven hours to Anchorage, Alaska, followed by an almost five-hour drive to Wonder Lake, to reach our destination. It was going to be a long-ass few days of travel. The first part of the flight went quickly. I watched a few movies and caught some shut-eye. I couldn't relax during the last leg. I needed to talk to my sister about what I saw back at the house. She was asleep beside me, but it was about time for her to wake up, anyway. I gave her a few shoves to wake her.

"Now would be a great time for you to drop the act and tell me what that really was, back at the house."

She looked at me like I had three heads, but the look on my face told her I wasn't going to let this go. With a long exhale, she finally responded.

"I promise you, Sissy, when we get to where we are going, I will explain everything. I can't do that now—there isn't enough time for the answers you seek. So please, just wait."

"I can't let it go for that long! I don't even know where Wonder Lake *is*. All you told me is how long it takes to get there."

"I know, Ry. Can you just wait, please?"

"Can I ask one thing?"

She sighed. "What is it, Ryan? I will answer it if I can."

"What I saw back at the house, how your hand was glowing. I can do that too, can't I?"

"I am so sorry, Ryan. You should have known about all of this so long ago. We couldn't get near you. We tried to come for you, Ry, I swear we did. Mom wouldn't let us. She is such a bitch for denying you the right to know the truth of—"

I cut her off —I had zero interest in this wait-and-see game. I just wanted a straight answer from her. The longer she took, the more anxious I got. I just wanted the truth, for once in my damn life.

"Truth about what, Stevie? I have a right to know. Just answer me, for God's sake."

Alex leaned across the aisle and eyed us both. "Now is not the time for this conversation, cousin. If you both could please keep the noise down, so we don't attract any more attention from the other passengers, it would be appreciated." As he finished, he shot Stevie a warning look that look shut us both up.

We spent the remainder of the flight quiet, occasionally making small talk with each other. I was still feeling antsy, needing answers from my sister. After the plane made its descent into LA, we left the aircraft to search for the boarding gate for our connecting flight to Alaska.

Once aboard the aircraft, we found our seats. Due to it being a smaller plane, we sat apart. Alex and Stevie were seated next to one another, with Chase and I a few rows behind. Once we got settled in our seats and fastened our belts, I leaned back in my chair and closed my eyes, intending to get some shut-eye. After the plane was in the air, Chase leaned over and whispered, "You will get all the answers you seek, cousin, once we get to Wonder Lake. I promise if Stevie does not tell you, I will."

I opened my eyes and moved slightly so I could look my cousin in the eye. There was no deceit behind his words; I knew Chase would spill the beans if Stevie didn't. I appreciated Chase so much in that moment.

"Thank you, Chase. I just don't want to be lied to anymore. I deserve to know." He gave me a warm smile and nodded. We spent the remainder of the flight in a comfortable silence. I couldn't stop thinking about what I had seen my sister do. I would glow blue if my emotions got the better and I never understood why. I need my sister to help me figure this all out and soon.

After departing the plane, we made our way out to the parking lot. Stevie had organized a hire car for our time we were here. We stuffed all our bags in the SUV then headed out for the long drive. We were a couple hours into our journey when I dozed off. I could feel the pull of my dream land awaiting me.

Chapter Five

I was walking through the woods, smiling up at the sky, when I felt the sensation of being watched. I stopped walking and scanned the area. He was here. I could feel him. I can't explain it, but I could always tell when Kai or Nico was near in my dream.

"I know you're out there, Kai. Why don't you just come out?" I turned when I heard a bush rustle behind me, then I saw him.

One of the most beautiful men I had ever seen in my life was stalking toward me. His skin was flawless, his body a work of God himself. He was shirtless, and had the kind of abs that men spend years trying to achieve. On him they just looked natural... meant to be. He had the most perfect set of teeth on display, and as I looked up to meet his gaze, I was drawn in by the most beautiful gray-blue eyes and was unable to look away. His hair was rumpled, a rich mix of brown with hints of blond.

"I have missed you, mi amor," he said as he lowered his head to kiss me. I opened for him immediately, like I always did, and he slipped his tongue inside my mouth. He pulled away after a few minutes with a smile on his face, leaving me breathless and panting. The sexual tension was palpable; I could feel my body heating with the need to have him inside me.

"That's one hell of a hello, Kai."

"I have missed you and have not seen you as much I would like." My dream guys were always so demanding. I never understood why—I mean, they were just dreams, after all, but it was so nice to feel needed and wanted by someone. Nico was the dominant one who always demanded my submission, while Kai was gentle and soft.

"I'm sorry," I said, feeling silly for saying that to someone who was just a figment of my imagination, but compelled to apologize all the same.

"Never be sorry, mi amor. I will take whatever time you give me."

I smiled at his sweet words. "Now that I am here, what would you like to do?"

"I wish we had time, mi amor, but you are nearly at your destination now, and I must get back. I will visit you soon and explain everything, I promise." What the hell was wrong with me? My dream guys were always weird, like they actually had somewhere else to be. Sometimes I wondered if my subconscious was trying to make them seem more real.

"Okay Kai, sure thing. Next time I want less talking and more body action." I would never say stuff like this to a real guy —I wasn't that kind of girl—but with my dream guys, I let my inner vixen out to play.

"Believe me, there will be no talking just you screaming my name, mi amor." His words sent shivers down my spine. He bent down and kissed me with such hunger that I swear I could have come just from kissing him. I put my hands around his neck and gripped the back of his hair, moaning into his mouth. I wanted him right here, right now. I needed him inside of me. I lowered my hands to undo his jeans, but he grabbed them and pulled away from me.

"There isn't enough time for that, mi amor, but rest assured I *will make it up to you next time." the smirk on his face telling me he knew what that kiss had done to me and he loved it.*

"Fine, but next time I might be the one playing hard to get," I said while still pouting at him.

"Go now, my love, and I will see you soon." Before I could respond, the darkness started to overtake me, but before I was fully out of my dream land, I heard Kai whispering, "Please try to understand and forgive me."

I woke to Stevie shaking me, a worried look on her face. I looked around and realized I was lying on the ground, the car parked haphazardly nearby, with Chase and Alex on either side of me with similarly anxious expressions on their faces.

"Why are you all looking at me like that? And why the hell am I on the ground?"

They all shared a look that I couldn't read. I felt once again as if I was being left out of a secret.

"You were shaking, and we tried to wake you, but you wouldn't wake up, so we got worried and stopped. What the hell happened?" Chase asked.

"I fell asleep." Geez, I didn't know being a deep sleeper was a crime. I didn't understand why they were freaking out.

"No, Ryan, you weren't just sleeping. You were shaking and glowing. What the hell happened when you were asleep?" Stevie demanded. Shit, I needed to figure out what the hell this glowing thing meant. It normally only happened when I was really angry or scared. I was actually starting to get worried, but I couldn't tell the others that.

"I was just having a weird dream, okay?" I obviously couldn't tell them that I was trying to seduce one of my dream lovers. I could feel the heat rising to my cheeks even thinking about mentioning such a thing.

"Tell me about the dream, Ryan, please," Alex pleaded, none the wiser as to the reason of my heated state.

"I would really rather not, but thanks for worrying," I said, hoping they would drop it.

"Ryan, come on" Chase urged.

"It was my dream, and if I don't want to tell you about it, I don't have to."

Chase let out a huff of air then looked me straight in the eyes.

"Well, when you start *glowing* in a public area, it then becomes *our* problem, but this isn't the place to talk about it, so let's get a move on and get to the cabin."

I nodded, knowing they weren't about to disclose any information they had on the whole glowing thing until we got to the cabin, and I was in no position to argue, given my refusal to discuss the dream, so I reluctantly got into the car.

Once we arrived at the cabin, the boys started unloading our bags and supplies, and I stood on the porch for a moment, taking in the view. To get to the cabin, you had to go along a dirt road that if you didn't know it was there, you would never find it. Thank God I wasn't driving. The cabin was surrounded by dense woods and very isolated; it would be the perfect place for someone who needed a break from real life.

The cabin was old, but sturdy by the look of it. It was a faded brown color, with dark green porch columns much like the color of the trees surrounding the house. The small porch on the front held two old rocking chairs that would be perfect to sit in and watch the sunset. I loved being here already and smelling the fresh air that the mountains and trees offered us.

As I was taking one last look around before heading inside, a shiver ran down my spine. It was that same feeling I had in my dream, of someone watching me. I felt a shiver run down my spine. I looked around the wooded area and saw nothing. Even so, I high-tailed it inside to find my sister and cousins.

As I entered the cabin, I was awestruck. The outside may have looked run down, but inside was like something from a magazine.

The entryway was decorated with antlers hanging on the wall, and just past that, the main living area held a beautiful set of gold and cream armchairs and a three-cushion couch. Next to that was the dining room and kitchen. The dining room was huge, with a long table fit for a castle, flanked by bench seats on either side.

"Close your mouth before a fly gets in there, squirt," Alex said with a laugh.

"Sorry, it's just I didn't expect it to look like this inside! You know, since the outside could use a refresh."

"Don't judge a book by its cover, cousin. All is not what it seems."

"Yeah, you can say that again. So, which one is my room?"

"Third door on the left, and there are towels in the hallway closet. Each room has its own en suite, so at least we don't have to hear you two girls fighting over the mirror," he said, smirking.

"Shut up, Alex, but thanks."

"You will love your room, it has a daybed and a great view of the landscape."

"How do you know that?" Alex looked around the room, searching for the others I assume. He finally pulled his gaze back to me and sheepishly replied.

"I saw it, when I put your bags in your room." *Okay*, I wasn't convinced, but I would let it go for now.

I set off down the hallway to find my room and wash away the couple of days of travel residue I could feel clinging to me. The room that was mine for our stay was the nicest room I'd ever stayed in. It had a massive, four poster king-sized bed in the middle of the room, with a bear skin rug at the foot of it. I had a beautiful view of the mountains, and right below the window was the day bed Alex had mentioned. I loved this place already. Tearing myself away from the view, I grabbed some clothes and headed into the bathroom for a quick shower. After that I was hunting down the others to get some answers and food. I needed both as soon as possible.

As I was leaving my room, I heard the others arguing, so I quietly shut my door so I could sneak down the hall and eavesdrop on their conversation. This was becoming a habit.

"She is going to want to know the whole story, Stevie." I could hear the irritation in Alex's voice.

"I will tell her everything she needs to know, especially if he is visiting her in her dreams now," my sister replied.

"We don't know for sure it is him she is dreaming of. But we can get the protection of the coven and the pack to keep her from him. But if he knows she is alive, he will be coming for her Stevie, and we all know that it's not an *if*, it's a *when*. So we need her to know now," Chase snapped.

"Keep your damn voice down. I have no idea how he would even know she exists. Dad made sure no one knew about her to keep her safe. I wonder how long he has been visiting her, if it is him?"

Alex butted in, "Long enough for her to feel the need to protect him from us. She doesn't want us to know that he visits her, and she doesn't even know who he is."

I came around the corner then, having had enough of all this talk behind my back. They needed to start telling me the truth, right now.

"I need to learn what? And who the fuck is coming for me?"

They all spun around in shock. Stevie pursed her lips, obviously annoyed that I had been listening in on their conversation, but I didn't care about her feelings right now.

"Why don't you have a seat, and we can start from the beginning and work our way up to the why and what, okay?" Chase was looking at me with pleading eyes, so I nodded and took a seat at the table next to Chase while Stevie and Alex sat on the other side.

"Okay, Ry, so you already know that we have been keeping something from you, but it wasn't because we wanted to. It's just that we didn't know how to tell you. It's not something you hear every day, and to be honest, it's not easy to explain either, so please just let us get it all out and then you can ask all the questions you want."

I nodded slowly. "Okay, I guess I can do that for you."

Stevie looked to both Alex and Chase, and they each gave her a nod. She let out a loud huff of air and then began.

"Ryan, you and I were born with...gifts, we'll call them, for argument's sake. I grew up knowing about mine, and how to use and channel my gift, because Dad taught me how."

"Wait—Dad knew about this? All of this glowing hands shit?" I exclaimed, cutting my sister off.

"No interrupting, I said! But yes, Dad did know. I am just going to come out with it—we're witches. Not like ride-around-on-broomstick witches...like cast spells kind of witches...we have powers."

Finally stunned speechless, I sat quietly, trying to put the pieces of my odd life together with the information I'd just received. Alex eyed me warily then nudged Stevie. She sighed, then asked.

"Are you okay?"

"I don't know what to think, or what I'm supposed to say to all this, Stevie. Alex, Chase—are you both witches?" I asked.

Alex and Chase both scoffed then pinned me with a glare.

"We are not witches. We are warlocks. Only women are called witches, Ry," Alex responded haughtily.

I nodded and rolled my eyes at their drama. As if being accidentally called the feminine version of something was a grave insult. Chase waved me off and Stevie gave me a sheepish smile.

"So, what does all this mean for me then?" I asked the group.

"It means that you have gifts and abilities, Sissy. They can help keep you safe. I know that this must be a lot to take in, and you should have been told about this a long time ago." My sister had an aura of sadness around her.

"Why was I never told about any of this? If Dad told you about all of this, and showed you how to use these *gifts*" I said with air quotes, "Why the hell was I kept in the dark?"

"Ryan, we tried to tell you..." Stevie started before I cut her off.

"Well, you didn't try hard enough! If what you say is true, then I could have protected myself, from her and all the bad shit she did to me! Instead you and Dad just gave up and left me with THAT FUCKING MONSTER!" I screamed.

I stood to leave, when Chase tried to put his hand on my shoulder. I shrugged him off and walked to the front door. I needed some air. I couldn't process what they were saying. Part of me couldn't comprehend any of it, but then the other half of me knew on some level that it was true. Whenever I was glowing, I always felt like I was a live wire. When my emotions got away from me, things would happen around me, things I couldn't explain—like the walls would rattle or the ground would shake, and things would go from one side of the room to the other.

Before I could continue with my thoughts, I heard a branch snap. I stopped dead in my tracks and realized I had walked so far into the woods that when I turned around, I couldn't see the cabin anymore. When I started to take a step toward the direction I came, a deep, husky voice froze me in place. Fear washed over me as I slowly turned to see who that voice belonged to.

"Hello," he said. He was huge, with intense brown eyes that stared at me so directly I wanted to look away. His hair was disheveled, and a few strands hung over his forehead. It was a light brown. He had this whole lumberjack look going on—he even wore a red and black flannel shirt with faded blue jeans that hugged him in all the right places. I didn't feel scared, like any normal person would have.

"Umm...hi?" It sounded like more of a question than I meant it to.

"You look lost?"

"I'm not lost. I was just taking a walk."

"Lie."

"Excuse me?" I snapped.

"You lied. Your heart rate picked up."

"What the fuck?" Is this fucking guy for real? How the hell could he hear my heartbeat?

"I'm sorry, I didn't mean to upset you Miss...?"

"Umm...Ryan. My name is Ryan."

"Well, Ryan, I did not mean to upset you, so I apologize."

"Thanks, that's okay. Look, I'm sorry. I shouldn't have cussed at you. It's just been one hell of a day, and I should really be heading back. The others will be getting worried. It was nice to meet you Mr..?"

"The pleasure was all mine, Miss Ryan, I'm sure I will see you around town sometime. Best get moving, it's getting cold."

He turned on his heel and walked back into the woods, heading away from my temporary home. I started walking back the way I came, thinking about the strange encounter I just had, and the fact that he hadn't answered my question about his name. After ten minutes, I emerged from the woods to find the others sitting outside on the porch. I approached them with my head held high. Chase and Alex stood from the two chairs on the porch, while Stevie remained seated on the steps. I exhaled loudly before addressing the group.

"I'm sorry I took off. I just needed to get some fresh air and clear my head. That was a big info dump."

"We understand," Chase replied with a sad smile

"No, you don't. This is hard for me to even believe, that you guys have grown up knowing all of this and being taught what you are. I have not had that luxury, and I wish I had. Stevie, I'm sorry for yelling at you. I know it wasn't your fault. I just feel like my life could have been so different if I had known. Maybe, if I did know, I could have protected myself. I always felt like a freak. Whenever my emotions would get out of control, I would glow, and I never knew why, but Mom hated it."

"I wish you had known, Ryan. I wish I knew what I know now, so that I could have come for you or tried to help you. I didn't know my specific gifts back then; if I did, I could have gotten you out. I am so sorry for what you have endured throughout your life. If I could have swapped places with you, I would have! I promise you, Ryan Gene Knox, that we will teach you what you need to know, so you never feel unprotected again. We will show you how to channel and harness your power. You are stronger than you know, Ry. So much stronger."

I looked into my sister's eyes and saw hope. She was proud of me for making it through my childhood with our mother. She didn't know our mother that well, but she had heard the stories I would tell her when I would sneak out to meet her.

"Stevie, it's not your fault..." I didn't get a chance to finish before Alex cut in.

"We have company."

Chase moved to stand in front me, as if to shield me from our visitor. Stevie and Alex stood on either side of Chase, their bodies coiled tight with tension. I didn't hear a car or even footsteps.

"Well, well, the infamous Knox family has returned." The man's voice sent shivers down my spine, and not in a good way, either. "Tell me, Miss Knox, where is your father? Surely the great Ralph Knox did not let his prized daughter come here alone, unprotected?"

The man's voice had a harsh edge to it, and you could tell from the condescending way he spoke my father's name that he hadn't liked him. I didn't understand why. This was the first time Stevie had been here, so how did he know her or my dad? Before I could think on it more, my sister spoke.

"Randall Cane, what an unpleasant surprise. What brings you to my family's land? You know your kind is not welcome here without invitation."

Wait, what did she just say—our family's fucking land? I'm missing something here, and I do not like it one bit. As soon as this Randall guy left, my sister was getting an earful from me. I was fucking done with the lies and the secrets. What else was my sister hiding from me?

"The fact that my clan was not notified of your return is what brought me here, young one. You would be wise to watch your tone. I do not care for smart-mouthed youth," he snapped. "Where is your father? We had an agreement, and your kind have not kept their end of the deal."

"My uncle is no longer with us, Cane. So watch how you speak of the dead!" Alex roared. I could feel the tension rolling off my three family members.

"My apologies, I did not know of his death. I meant no disrespect, young ones. Your father was a great man, Miss Knox. He brought peace to all the communities, but I am afraid that peace may not last much longer, given recent events." Randall sounded like he was trying really hard to project sincerity, but he failed miserably to pretend he wasn't also happy our father was dead.

"What do you mean? The peace treaty has had no problems as far as we are aware. Our coven has been keeping tabs on the witches and warlocks in our region," Chase stated.

"Then they have misled you, Mr. Knox. I can assure my kind and the packs have been under attack for the past three months. We assume it's the coven, as it's not my clan or the pack. If you cannot reel your coven in, we will take matters into our own hands."

"Is that a threat, Cane?" Chase snapped, stepping off the porch stairs, heading toward Randall. His fists were balled at his sides, with a purple light covering them. No sooner had Chase moved—and I came into view—did the strange man take a step back, almost like he had seen a ghost. He looked scared.

"It cannot be! You cannot be alive—she said you were dead!" I was meant to be dead? Chase stopped in his tracks and peered over his shoulder at me, clearly no better informed than I about this development. I shrugged and decided to ask Randall myself. I wasn't going to hide anymore, or be lied to and kept in the dark.

"What do you mean *I'm supposed to be dead?* And who is this 'she'?"

He shook his head before he answered; it was as if he was trying to clear his mind of what he was thinking. He was not a tall man—Chase and Alex towered over him. He had blond hair and blue eyes, and his build was stocky. If he hadn't been projecting malice and rage like an antenna, I might have even described him as attractive.

"Forgive me, I am Randall Cane, king of the Alaskan Vampire Clan," he said with a bow.

My mouth charged ahead before my brain could catch up. "What the fuck did you just say? Vampires? Are you kidding me?" Randall turned to Stevie with eyes sparking in outrage.

"My sister is new to all of this," Stevie rushed to add, giving me a sharp look. Her irritation pissed me off. How dare she? It wasn't *my* fault I didn't know about this shit.

"Sister? Well that explains why you look alike." he said dryly. "Why have I never heard of her before? Ralph never said he had two daughters."

"That is not of your concern, Randall!" Stevie's voice was like a knife, razor-sharp.

"It *is* my concern when I signed a blood treaty with a man who lied to me, and told me he had one living heir, not two!" he roared.

"You will watch your tone when you address the coven heir, Cane. If she says it is not your concern, then it's not," Alex bellowed and took a step forward.

"You will watch how you address me, Mr. Knox. Do not forget your place here. I will end you if you push me too far, boy!"

"You lay one hand on my cousin, and I will kick your ass to kingdom come, buddy. I may not have the witchy voodoo shit under control like they do, but I am a black belt in karate," I snapped at the vampire king. Nobody was talking to my cousin like that in my presence.

All heads turned in my direction. Stevie looked shocked, while Alex and Chase were suppressing smug grins.

Randall guffawed, which sent my blood pressure rising.

Once his fit of giggles finally stopped, he looked to me and spoke.

"There will be no need for that, Miss...?"

"My name is Ryan."

"Well, I guess your father was telling the truth. He said your mother really did want a boy." The sarcasm was thick in his tone.

He was actually right about that. My mother hated the fact that we were not boys. She said girls were always trouble, and boys were easier, because they could never come home with a baby growing in their womb.

"Well, surprise! I'm a girl, just like my sister, tits and all," I replied, with a wink and fake smile.

"You have the mouth of a sailor to boot. It's a pleasure to meet you, Miss Ryan. I hope you will be staying in town for a while? I would love to get to know you better."

"That's not going to happen. If you want to talk to her, then you can do so in front of all of us." Chase's tone left no room for argument, and his glare would have sent me back a step or two if it had been directed my way.

"Well, if that is the case, I would love for you all to join me this evening at my home. I am having a little get-together. The pack will be over for a meeting regarding the treaty, so it would be beneficial for you all to join us."

"Wait! What do you mean *pack*? As in, like, a werewolf pack?" I said, laughing. Next thing you know, they're going to produce Santa Claus at this meeting.

"I do not understand why you think the pack is funny. They are hairy, ugly creatures, but they are no laughing matter." Randall seemed bemused by me, tilting his head to the side.

"Holy fuck, you're for real. There is a wolf pack?" I can't believe this; my mind is reeling with all the shit I have learned today. This was some *Twilight* shit, was Randall going to sparkle in the sunlight?

Stevie turned to me and murmured, "We will explain everything, Ry—we just haven't had the chance yet." Stevie then turned back to Randall. "We accept your invitation, Randall."

"Excellent. Please arrive no later than seven this evening. Until then, I will bid you farewell, Knox family." And with a slight bow, he turns and is gone like a flash of light. I scan the yard, unable to believe my eyes. It was like he just vanished into thin air. I didn't even notice Alex approaching me, I was so stunned by Randall's vanishing act.

"How you holding up, squirt?"

"I feel like I should be in a looney bin," I deadpanned.

"With padded white walls?" Chase teases, a playful smirk on his face.

"Yep," I agreed.

"I know you must have a lot of questions for us, and we want to answer them all. For your own wellbeing, though, we can't right now. We have to get ready for this evening's event. Can you handle waiting a little bit longer?" Alex asked.

I didn't really know how to answer that question. I wanted answers, and I had so many questions, but I needed time to process what I had just learned today. So I simply shrugged and nodded in agreement. With that, we all went inside to begin getting ready for an evening with vampires and werewolves— whatever that entailed.

Chapter Seven

While standing in the shower, letting the water rinse away the day, I couldn't stop my mind from going over all that I had learned, not only about myself, but my family and even the world as I knew it. I would never have thought that a family could keep such secrets from each other. I finally gave up on trying to piece the puzzle which was my life together, and sighed and got out of the shower. I put my robe on and left my hair in a towel, deciding it was best to worry about my unruly mane later. As I was going through my bags, I realized I didn't have anything suitable to wear. Or at least I didn't think so. I'd never been to a party with witches, warlocks, vampires and werewolves. I was just working up the nerve to go ask about the dress code when someone starts knocking on my door. Without waiting for an invitation, the door opened and my sister poked her head in.

"Jesus, Stevie, I'm not even dressed yet."

"Oh please, Sissy, we're identical twins. I see what you have every day when I look in the mirror!" She snorted at my prudishness, and I let out a huff and waved her in.

"I have nothing appropriate to wear to dinner, Stevie. I don't think I can go in skinny jeans and a T-shirt."

"No, you probably can't, but you can wear this," she said, handing me the most beautiful dress. It's a deep blue, with a plunging neckline. It had two slits down the sides that stopped just below your panties. When she turned the dress around, I saw that it had no back, and realized that underwear would not be an option in a dress like that.

"Stevie, there is no way in hell I can wear that. I'm not you. I can't pull off a dress like that."

"Shut up, Ryan! I don't want to hear that shit come out of your mouth. You are beautiful, and you will wear this dress. Don't knock it til you try it on. I bought it a while ago and never had a chance to wear it, so I want to give it to you." I knew by the look in her eyes I wasn't going to win this argument.

Sighing, I got up and took the dress from her, heading into the bathroom to change. Once I finally got the dress on, I refused to look in the mirror, knowing that if I saw what I looked like, I might take it off. When I finally emerged from the bathroom, I looked to my sister, and her mouth was hanging open. A blush started burning its way up my neck. I never wore things like this in real life—only in my dreams.

"Is it really that bad? I told you I couldn't pull it off, Stevie." I was about to take the damn thing off when Stevie grabbed my arm.

"Don't you dare! You look beautiful, Ry, and I mean it. I just can't believe you don't see how beautiful you are."

Her words brought tears to my eyes; my mother always said I was hideous. The only time I ever felt truly beautiful was when I was in my dreams with the guys. They made me feel like a goddess. I only started to view myself as something more than trash when I started to have dreams with Kai and Nico in them.

They would always tell me I'm beautiful and my beauty shined from within me.

"When you grow up hearing how ugly you are all the time, you start to believe it," I whispered, my head hung low. Stevie grabbed me by the chin and lifted my head so we were eye to eye.

"You will never look down at yourself again, do you hear me? I will not have it. You are a fucking coven heir, Ryan! You look down to no one. –Tonight you will hold your head high and handle yourself like the royalty you are. Do you hear me? If you don't, they will see you as weak, and you will become their prey. Always keep eye contact and never let them know how they make you feel."

"I don't understand what you're saying, Stevie."

"If they know you are scared, they will prey on that weakness. The Knox coven is the strongest in the world, and we cannot be seen as anything other than that. If you have to fake it til you make it, that's what you will do. Randall may seem harmless, but he is not, and neither is the pack. We must show strength in the eyes of our enemies—you understand?"

It was clear there was a lot more to what she was saying than what I knew, but I was going to try the whole "fake it til you make it" thing, starting now. I gave my sister a tight smile and nodded.

"Okay, now let's do your hair and makeup!" She said with a clap of her hands. Dear Lord, save me now.

An hour later, we were walking out of my room to get the boys and be on our way to Randall's little gathering.

"Yowza! Look at you two. Ryan, you look absolutely beautiful." Chase was such a charmer, but his words gave me a small boost in confidence. I refused to let my family down. I was going to make them proud tonight.

"You both really do look great, but if we don't hurry up, we're going to be late, and that will be a problem," Alex said while holding the front door open.

After a forty-five minute drive through forest and gravel roads, we approach two massive iron gates held up by huge brick pillars. On top of the pillars sat two gargoyles whose grimaces were just plain creepy. Alex pulled up next to an intercom and hit a button. After a moment, a man's voice came over the speaker.

"Cane Manor."

"Alex Knox, from the Knox coven. We have been invited here this evening by Mr. Cane." I can hear the distaste in Alex's voice when he says Randall's name.

"Yes, sir, please drive through."

No sooner had the man finished speaking then the gates opened and we drove through. The driveway has trees lining the drive all the way up to the house. As we get closer, I saw a fountain in front of the house, its presence creating a roundabout for drivers. The fountain itself is a beautiful work of art. It had four horses rearing up, almost like they were fighting. The horses were shooting water from their mouths, spotlights were pointed at the fountain. It was clearly the centre piece of the front yard.

The house—I mean, it wasn't even a house, more like an estate—was huge; it reminded me of the White House. It had the same four big pillars out the front, windows were scattered all over the front of the mansion, there was an American flag placed on the roof as well. The White House seemed more welcoming then Randall's mansion though. The entrance to the home had guards stationed outside of it. Or at least I assumed they are guards. I was a bit nervous about coming here before, but now I was about to burst out of my skin from nerves. I mean, who has armed guards at the door besides pop stars and presidents?

Alex finally eased the car to a stop, and he and Chase started to climb out. I grabbed Stevie's hand.

"Why are there guards?" I whispered.

"Because he is the vampire King, not just *a* king—he is *the* king." My face must look like a mask of horror, as she gives my hand a reassuring squeeze. "We're here with you, Ry. You are not alone. No one will harm you. If they even look at you wrong, let us know, and they will be taken care of. We may be young, but we are not weak. *You* are not weak."

With that, said she slipped out of the back seat to join the boys. I took one last deep breath and did the same. Chase offered me his arm, and I linked mine through his and gave him a nervous smile. He patted my arm and gave me a wink. Alex and Stevie led the way. As we approached the stairs leading to the front door, I start worrying I might trip and break my ankle. I was never any good at wearing heels, but Stevie insisted I wear them because, "Converse were not acceptable to wear with a dress." I felt like everything was on display: my back was bare; my breasts were just barely covered. The slits up the sides were making me worry if a gust of wind came, everyone would be able to see the G-string I had on.

As we reached the top of the stairs, Alex gave the guards a curt nod. The guards opened the two massive wooden front doors, and immediately I am assaulted by classical music and voices and laughter. I don't know what I was expecting, but this wasn't it. The foyer is beautiful. There are wooden floors throughout, with stunning furs lying on the floor. I had a brief pang of sadness for the animals that had worn those beautiful skins in life, and hoped they had not been killed simply for their fur. I loved animals and found value in all life.

As we neared the end of the hall, Alex and Stevie made a left turn into the main area, where the people had gathered. As Chase and I rounded the corner, I stopped dead in my tracks. There were people everywhere! The women were in ball gowns that looked like they were from the 1800s, but they made them look so glamorous and relevant to this era. And though the dresses were elaborate, no clothing could dull their radiant beauty. They were flawless.

The men wore tuxes like Alex and Chase, but there were cravats and elaborately embroidered vests and all manner of colors and fabrics. The men were just as beautiful as the women in their own way. They knew it, too—you could tell by the way they sauntered around the room like they owned it. A server passed by with a tray full of champagne, and I grabbed one, thinking the alcohol would calm my nerves. Just as I was about to take a sip, a hand snaked around me and nabbed the glass right out of my hand. I froze, and the stranger came around to face me—it was the man from the woods.

He stood there, calmly sipping my champagne, a smirk on his unreasonably handsome face. My breath caught in my throat. He looked delicious when I saw him earlier today, but now, done up in his tux, he was a whole meal. Gone was the lumberjack-looking hunk and hello, Mr. Sexy. His hair was slicked back out of his face, and my God, those chocolate brown eyes! They could peel the clothes off any woman. He had a five o'clock shadow marking his jawline, and he made not shaving look like a new trend. His tux fitted him like a glove and showed his well-defined muscles. Chase broke the tension-filled silence.

"Jax. What can I do for you this evening?" Irritation was clear in his voice. Jax. I was irrationally pleased to have a name for my mystery lumberjack.

"Chase, I didn't realize you were in town. Did any of the others return as well?" he asked, his eyes never moving off me.

"We're all here, Marshall, so I suggest you take a step back from Ryan and remove your eyes from her, before I do it for you," Chase snapped.

"So, she's yours then?"

"That is not of your concern now, is it?" I could hear the underlying threat in Chase's voice. Why did my cousin not like Jax?

"When you bring a stranger onto my lands and you have no claim on her, it becomes my business. She doesn't smell like one of you." My hackles rise as they continue to speak about me like I'm not even here. Rude much?

"As you can see, jackass, she is Stevie's twin sister. If you can't know that from looking at her, then you're more fucked in the head than I thought. She has just as much right to be here as you do, pup."

"Pup?" Jax let out a throaty growl. "Boy, I am no *pup*; I can assure you of that."

I knew things were getting out of hand when Chase grabbed my arm and started pulling me behind him. I don't know why he felt so much anger toward Jax, and I didn't think now was the time to ask. I yanked my arm from Chase's grip and stepped between the two brooding males that looked like they were about to tear each other apart.

"My name is Ryan. As you already know, Chase is my cousin. I don't know why you two don't like each other, and at this point in time, I don't give a shit." I then turned to Chase and said "Dial it down a notch, big guy. We just got here, and I don't want to get kicked out. Let's go get me another glass of something to help me get through this, okay?"

Chase gave me a stiff nod while still pinning Jax with a death glare. Just as we were turning to walk away, Jax put a hand on my shoulder.

"I'm sorry, I didn't mean to ruin your evening. It's just that you don't have the same scent as the others. You are different, and in this world, different can be dangerous."

Chase was standing beside me, seething, ready to throw the first punch if Jax didn't let my arm go. Noticing Chase's discomfort, Jax let his hand slide off my shoulder.

"Look, dude—"

"My name is Jackson Marshall, but my friends call me Jax," he said, smiling.

"Okay—*Jax*. I just got here, and I don't know a lot about what the hell the others do, okay? So if you could just back off and stop freaking smelling me, that would be great." With that said, I turned on my sky-high heels and headed out to find my sister. Tonight was going to be a damn long night if this shit kept up.

Chapter Eight

After leaving Jax and finding another server, Chase and I grabbed a glass each this time and made our way out to the back patio in search of Stevie and Alex. I couldn't help but stop and take in the yard. It was like a fairy tale. There were candles along the ground, lighting up the pathways. A fountain sat in the middle of the yard, a twin of the one out front.

Small shrubbery bushes lined the paths, and a dream-like white pergola sat at the end of the pathway. I never thought vampires would have a yard like this. I spotted Stevie in the pergola with a few others. I could only tell it was my sister because she was wearing an off-the-shoulder yellow dress—she stood out like Big Bird. That was Stevie—she loved being center of attention.

As we were walking toward the pergola, I once again had the sensation of being watched. I scanned the yard, but no one was looking our way. I knew there were lots of people here, but I just couldn't shake the feeling that a predator was lurking in the shadows.

"There you two are! We lost you as soon as we got here," Alex said, shaking me out of my inner thoughts.

"We got stopped by that dick Jackson Marshall," Chase grumbled, still tense from the encounter.

"What the hell did he want?" Stevie snapped.

"To ask about Ryan and why she smelt funny."

"Shut up! I don't smell! He's just weird. Hot, but weird." I swear I heard a growl coming from the forest as I spoke. This paranoia was ridiculous.

"Stay away from him, Ry. His kind doesn't like us." Alex always had to be so cryptic.

"Actually, that reminds me—you told him your name and then said 'but you already know that.' How would he know that, Ry?" Chase asked.

"I met him earlier today, when I took off to clear my head. He was in the woods," I replied sheepishly, feeling like I had done something wrong. How was I supposed to know who to talk to and who not to?

"That fucker was on our land? What the hell?" Alex hissed.

Stevie shushed him. "Now is not the place to worry about this. We don't know how far Ry wandered; their lands do back onto ours. She could have crossed the boundary. We need to find Randall and sort out whatever he has to tell us, and then let's get the fuck out of here," Stevie said with a grim look.

With that done, the four of us went in search of the vampire king.

After making our way back inside and maneuvering through the crowds of people, Stevie lead us down the hallway near where we entered. We stopped outside a large wooden door. Alex knocked and we waited to be invited in.

"Enter!" a voice shouted from behind the door.

Alex opened the door, and we all filed in. The room was decorated in rich browns and maroon, with oil paintings in elaborate gilded frames. The fire was lit, and above the mantle there was a portrait of a woman in a lavender gown, with a small hat atop her head. Her face was fanned with black curls and her skin was luminescent, even in a painting. She had the most rich and vibrant violet eyes. They reminded me of Nico's. I heard someone cough and turned to see Randall standing behind a massive oak desk. Behind him were floor to ceiling windows that perfectly framed the view of the forest and mountains. He waved us over to the other side of the room, where there were two couches and two single chairs that looked more like thrones than living room furniture.

"Please take a seat, and we can discuss some matters," Randall instructed I let out a snort when he took one of the single chairs at the end. Stevie shot me a death glare, so I quickly masked my snort by coughing.

"What are the matters you would like to discuss, Mr. Cane?" Alex asked, adopting a blasé tone.

"First, why was I not notified of your uncle's death? And why was I never told that Ralph Knox's other daughter survived?"

"I was planning on telling you my father had passed, once we arrived and got settled in. Rest assured, Mr. Cane, we were not leading you astray. Also, my sister was not raised with my father and me, so he thought it wise not to let anyone know that she was alive, since she was not under his protection. She lived with our mother," Stevie stated.

Randall sat on his throne, scratching his chin like he was deep in thought. He turned his eyes to me, and I forced myself to meet his gaze, head up, as Stevie had demanded.

"Did you know of any of this, Miss Knox?"

I didn't know how to answer that question appropriately, so I thought telling the truth was the best option.

"Mr. Cane, this is all new information to me, like my sister just said. I was raised by our mother. I had no idea about any of this"—I waved my hands around— "magic stuff, until this morning." He looked like he had just won the lottery. That wasn't creepy or anything.

"I understand, Miss Knox, I really do. However, your father should have told us about you. It changes things with the treaty, you being alive and present in our midst." I was about to respond when the door swung open and Jax strolled in. What the hell was he doing here?

"Sorry I'm late! You forgot to let me know the meeting was starting." Jax was pinning Chase with a death glare. Chase just smiled.

Jax took a seat on a couch and asked, "What did I miss?" Randall filled him in, and Jax seemed to have trouble hiding his shock at my ignorance.

"Why were you kept a secret?" he asked me.

"I wasn't a secret, as far as I knew," I told him with a shrug.

"Ryan was not raised with us, so she was not mentioned for her own safety," Stevie snapped.

"Just because she grew up somewhere else does not give you and your father the right to LIE TO ME!" Randall roared. I sank back into the couch cushions and started counting the possible exits.

"No one lied to you, Randall. We were all children when the treaty was renewed. None of us were involved, so if Ryan's existence being kept from you is a problem, we cannot help that. The one who could answer that question is now dead," Alex fired back at Randall.

"Look, we're all a bit on edge having your cousin here. Having two heirs is unheard of, so you can see why we are a bit upset about all this," Jax said, looking sympathetic.

"What's so bad about having two heirs?" I asked to no one in particular.

Jax shared a look with Randall, and then they both looked to my sister and cousins, as if waiting for one of them to answer my question. With a sigh, Stevie finally answered.

"An heir is someone who is next in line to rule. In our case, being an heir means one of us is in line to rule the Knox coven. Because you do not yet know how to wield your powers, I will step up to rule our people until you are ready. Then we can sort what happens next." I could tell by the look on my sister's face that she was eager to take on that leadership role, which was fine by me. I knew there was more to it, Stevie was withholding information. Once again I was being put in a situation I didn't understand, by the people who supposedly loved me.

"You know what? I never asked for this shit, Stevie, any of it! And I don't want it." As I stood up to leave, the office door opened once more, and in walked the last person I thought I would ever see in life. I couldn't breathe. I couldn't move. Then it all went dark.

As I was coming to, I braced myself for the inevitable pain from hitting the floor, but it never came. My head was resting on something soft. I heard the others fussing around me, wondering if I was okay. As I opened my eyes to try tell everyone I was fine. The first thing I see, Is beautiful blue-gray eyes, I know those eyes they belong to Kai. My dream man was real, He was holding me in his lap. My breaths were coming out in short fast pants; I thought my heart might jump out of my chest. I tried to open and close my eyes a few times to make sure I wasn't dreaming, but he stayed right where he was.

As he was leaning his head down to look at me, I realized my head was resting within an inch of his manhood. I couldn't help the blush that spread across my cheeks. I tried to sit up, but he put his hand in the middle of my chest to stop me, and in the quietest whisper, he spoke to me.

"I would never let you fall, mi amor." Holy fuck, he is real. I couldn't wrap my head around that. He called me 'mi amor,' so that must mean he was really in my dreams, right? But how?

I looked at him, at a loss for words which was a rare thing for me. I had been dreaming about this man for years and now here he is, holding me.

"Thank God you're okay," Chase breathed, kneeling down beside me. He started to slide his hands under my arms so he could lift me up, but my beautiful dream god growled. I snapped my head back toward him and gaped—he had his lips pulled back and his fangs out. Yes, I said fangs! My dream guy was real and he was a...vampire? I am clearly fucked in the head. The dude has fangs, and I'm sitting here swooning over him.

He looked down at me, and his eyes told me what he couldn't. He was ashamed of himself and his actions. He clamped his mouth shut, as if to hide his fangs, and turned his head away. Out of sheer instinct, I reached out and turned his face toward me so I could look him in the eyes.

"Don't hide from me," I said firmly. He had nothing to be ashamed of. I mean I'm a fucking witch—so what if he is a vampire? Before he could respond, my sister spoke.

"Let go of my sister now, enforcer. If you harm her, I will end you." Stevie had so much hatred in her tone that it made me gasp.

I was about to say something to protect my dream man, but before I could, Kai had me on my feet in a flash. He had his hands on my hips to steady me, but it also felt like he didn't want to let me go. I couldn't help but remember my dreams— were they real? I tilted my head back so I could ask him the one question burning a hole in my head.

"Who are you?"

"My name is Melakai Cane, Miss Knox. I am the head of the vampire king's enforcers." He had a look of regret on his beautiful face. He was being so formal. I didn't like it. Where was my relaxed sex god, who always made me laugh?

"Kai, step away from her now, before you do something you will regret," Jax warned Melakai, taking a step toward us.

"You take one step closer, Jackson, and you and I will finish what we started years ago—right here, right now," Kai growled at Jax.

"Melakai, son. Step away from the girl," the king ordered. Son? Wait, did that mean Randall was his dad?

With a final look at me to make sure I was okay, he took his hands off my hips. I felt instantly cold without his touch to warm me. I didn't want him to let me go. I wanted him to hold me forever. He was real, and I needed to know if he was really in my dreams. I have never been one to be like this toward a guy, but I just couldn't help the pull I felt toward him, like my life force was telling me to hold onto him. I have never felt safe in my life except when Kai was holding me. After stepping away from me, Kai made his way over to stand by the king. Stevie came rushing over and gave me a bone-crushing hug.

"What the hell was that, Ry?" she asked, looking me over for injuries, I guess.

"I don't know. Sorry for worrying you. I should have had something to eat before having that glass of champagne, I guess." I couldn't tell her the truth about Kai being one of my dream guys. I don't know why, but I felt like Kai being in my dreams was something I needed to keep private. Glancing over at Kai and seeing the look on his face, I knew I made the right decision.

"Now, can we all have a seat and try this again? I would like to finish our discussion," the king barked.

"Sounds good to me, but why is he here?" Jax asked, nodding toward Melakai.

"He's my heir and my son." Oh, so he *is* the king's son. "He has every right to be here, Mr. Marshall. Do not ever question my leadership or my sons again. Do I make myself clear?" Randall said, pointing a stern look Jax's way. Kai had a look of disdain plastered on his face, but he quickly masked it. That look was pointed at Randall, not Jax.

With a nod of his head, Jax took his seat and the rest of us followed. The door opened again, and in walked a huge man, around the size of a big bear. He had a ginger beard, shoulder-length red hair, and brown eyes. He wore dark jeans, a black button-up shirt, and my God, was the shirt tight! If he flexed his biceps, he would tear the shirt. He gave us a nod and smiled at my sister then went to stand beside Jax.

"Since your second-in-command is here, I thought mine should be as well. Everyone, this is Tyler. He is my Beta," Jax told the group. Stevie couldn't keep her eyes off Jackson's Beta. I gave her a nudge so she would close her mouth.

"Pleasure to meet you all," he said with a bow of his head.

"No, no the pleasure is all mine," Stevie said with a wink.

I couldn't help it; I started laughing my ass off. Alex and Chase joined in as well. The king gave me a dirty look, but fuck him and the stick up his ass. Stevie punched me in the arm to shut me up, but Melakai didn't seem to like that. He took a step forward and pinned my sister with a glare.

"You would be wise to never lay your hands on her again, Coven heir," Kai spat.

I stopped laughing immediately, as did the others. Stevie stood up to square off against Kai. Oh no, this wasn't going to end well.

"You would do well to know your place, enforcer. Do not ever interfere in my family business again. It's coven *queen* now," she hissed. I felt like I was missing something here. Everyone seemed to have ill feelings toward Kai, and I didn't understand why.

"Why doesn't everyone stop hating on the poor guy and get

on with this talk, so I can go and get something to eat." Kai had a look of pride in his eyes that look sent butterflies to my tummy. He could always set my body on fire with just one look in my dreams, now he could also do it in real life.

"Tyler and I can take you ladies out for something to eat after this. Their kind doesn't eat real food." I could hear the dig in Jax's voice—he clearly only said that to piss Kai off.

"You will not be going anywhere with her, dog," Kai snapped back.

"Is that a threat, you leech?" Jax sneered back. Both men took a step toward each other. I quickly stood and jumped between them.

"Thanks, guys, but I'm a big girl, I can make my own decisions, and I'd rather just go home and eat there. So let's get this show on the road." I couldn't tell everyone the truth, that I would rather go out with Kai.

Both men then stepped back, and Jax took his seat. I took my seat next to Stevie. Chase and Alex had smiles on their faces. I shot them both a dirty look; I knew what they were smiling about. They knew I was attracted to Kai.

"Now that the pissing contest is out of the way for Ryan's attention, let's talk about the treaty," Alex said, still grinning. I went beet-red from embarrassment; he was *so* getting punched for that comment when we leave.

"I would like a new treaty drawn up with new terms," the king stated.

That was it. Everyone stood up and started shouting over each other. The whole room was in uproar. Before anyone knew what was happening, the door burst open, and guards came piling in. One grabbed Stevie, and Alex went to lunge for him, but was caught mid-air by another guard. Chase went to help his brother, but was restrained by another guard. These guys were coming out of nowhere. Jax went to grab my arm and was stopped by a fist to the face—Kai's fist to be exact. Then they were all-out brawling on the floor. Tyler couldn't help Jax as he was subdued by three guards.

I was trying to help the others when a guard grabbed me from behind. I screamed, and Stevie started shouting threats at the guard to let me go or she would tear him limb from limb. I don't know what happened: maybe it was the rush of fear I was feeling, but my body felt really hot, and then out of nowhere, blue light shot from my hands at the guard that was holding me. He dropped to the floor. Stevie had a look of utter shock on her face.

I looked around the room and realized everyone had stopped fighting—they were all staring at me. My hands were still glowing, and I felt like a live wire.

"She is the one," the king said with awe in his voice, almost like he had found the missing puzzle piece.

"Ryan, look at me. Relax, Sissy, just breathe, everything is going to be okay," my sister said, trying to shake out of the guards hold. He reluctantly let her go and took a step toward me, but I stepped back out of her reach.

"How the fuck is this all okay, Stevie? I'm a freak! Look at me! I'm fucking glowing, and I just hurt SOMEONE!" As I screamed the last word, a blast of blue light shot out from me. The force was so great it shattered the windows and blew out the fire in the fireplace. I couldn't control the rage coursing through my veins. All the feelings I had bottled up, and the anger I had pushed deep down inside of me, from the years of torture as a child, were trying to break free. It brought everyone in the room to their knees— except for Kai.

Melakai made his way over to me, pushing against the power I was pulsing out. I could see the strain on his face as he struggled to get to me. When he finally stood in front of me, he cupped my face in both his hands and spoke so softly.

"Mi amor, it's okay, you are safe. Just breathe. Let me help you. I can make it stop. Just let me help you," he begged. I knew in that moment I could trust him to make it stop, so I nodded. He closed the sliver of space between us and pulled me into a tight embrace, whispering, "Sleep, mi amor." With his words, everything just stopped and went dark.

Chapter Ten

I awoke on the edge of the lake. Sitting up, I looked to my side, and sure enough, Kai was sitting next to me. This was our other dream land. The lake was so beautiful and calm. It was my favorite place to be, surrounded by trees and mountains. Knowing Kai is now a real person and not a figment of my imagination, I felt shy and unsure.

"Where are we?" I asked.

"At Lake William, mi amor."

"I got that part, Kai; I mean is this place even real?"

"Yes."

"Are you going to tell me where this place is located?"

"You can find Lake William hidden in the mountains in Alaska. I found this place many years ago, with my brothers." I was determined to find Lake William now. I didn't want to waste any more time talking about the lake.

"So you're real?"

"I am as real as you are."

"Okay...so how are we here, and why are we here?"

"I brought you here so your mind could relax. I know this is your favorite place, so I thought bringing you here would help.

Your power was too much for you, and you couldn't control it. So I helped you."

I remembered that he had offered to help me after I hurt that guard and blew the office apart.

"I hurt that man and destroyed the office. I didn't mean to hurt him. I don't even know how I did it! It just happened," I wailed.

"He's a vampire. He will heal fast, and he will not die."

Thank God for that. I don't know if I could live with myself if I had killed him. At the time, I didn't care what happened. It was like I wasn't myself.

"I'm sorry, I lost it back there. This is all just too much for me. Finding out I'm a witch and then that you are real. I mean, holy shit—like, this is mind-blowing stuff." Kai leaned over and tucked a tendril of hair behind my ear. I felt my body starting to heat from his touch. His voice distracted me from my thoughts.

"I can't begin to try and understand what you are going through, but just know I will be here to help you along the way, mi amor. I am sorry for letting you believe I was not real."

"What happened in my dreams—" He cut me off before I could finish.

"All of it was real, all of it," he said with a devilish grin.

"Oh my God!" I started blushing, feeling so embarrassed about everything that we had done and the things I had said to him. "I'm a virgin," I blurted out. Fucking smooth Ryan, real smooth. Kai started laughing.

"I beg to differ, mi amor," he said through breaks in his laughter. His laugh was like music to my ears. I loved that sound so much.

"How is this possible? Are you telling me that my dream sex is all fucking real?" God strike me down now; this has got to be the most embarrassing moment of my life.

He tilted his head to the side and pressed his lips in a tight line, like he was trying not laugh at me again.

"Yes and no. After all, it is still just a dream. Your physical body has not been touched by a man in the real world, just in your dream world."

"Why didn't you tell me you were real? After everything we have done and the things I have said, you could have told me." I couldn't look him in the eye. I behaved like a ravenous hussy in my dreams.

He laughed at me, again! I couldn't stop the smile that spread across my face. He looked so relaxed and carefree. I didn't really know the real him, but in person he seemed like the type that was always serious and on guard. I wanted so badly to know the real him and what made him happy.

"I'm glad that my embarrassment amuses you, Mr. Cane."

He immediately stopped laughing, all traces of humor wiped from his beautiful face. I didn't know what I said to upset him so badly.

"Please don't call me that; I do not wear that name because I have a choice."

"I'm sorry, I didn't mean to offend you." I hung my head, not wanting him to see the confusion on my face. I don't know why his name upset him, but I didn't want him to be angry with me.

"Never turn those eyes away from me, mi amor." I snapped my eyes back up to him. His voice had such a command in it that I knew not to defy him. He always demanded eye contact when we had sex in my dream. I loved staring at him while he pounded into me. Oh God, I needed to stop thinking of that right now. Judging by the smirk on his face, he knew exactly where my mind had drifted. His eyes were burning with desire, and I couldn't look away. My nether region was getting slick, just by the way he was looking at me. He raised his hand to my face and pulled me close. I could feel the sexual tension building between us. I closed my eyes, waiting for his lips to crash against mine. I wanted him to take me right here, right now. Instead he pulled back and dropped his hand. I snapped my eyes open, not knowing what the hell made him stop. I needed him to relieve the ache between my thighs.

"We must go, mi amor. The others are awaiting our return." Before I could answer, he grabbed my hand, and I felt a whoosh of wind—then nothing.

Chapter Eleven

I felt someone shaking me, and heard my name being called. I didn't want to wake up. I was having the best dream ever. Then I realized it wasn't a dream; Melakai was here and I wanted to jump his bones again in my dream. Holy fuck! I was acting like a hussy. I got so turned on in my dream that I could feel the pool of liquid between my thighs. I had to find a way to not dream anymore—to block him out somehow. I snapped my eyes open to see Stevie leaning over me with worry lines marring her face.

"Thank fuck, Sissy. I was about to stake his vampire ass if he didn't bring you back from wherever the fuck he took you," she said. I'm a terrible person. Here's my sister, worried about me, and I'm in a dream trying to screw Kai.

"I'm okay, Stevie, I swear." Well, except for the fact that I was feeling needy and hot, thanks to Kai.

"You smell like you're more than okay to me," Tyler retorted, a look of disgust prominent on his face.

"What the fuck is that supposed to mean, jackass?" Chase snapped.

"Ask your new coven queen—she knows," Tyler smugly replied.

I could feel all eyes on me in that moment. Surely he didn't mean he scented my arousal, right? Judging by the look on Jackson's face, I was starting to think they *could* smell my arousal. Before the tension-filled silence could continue, Kai spoke.

"She needs to be trained—her power is too great for her to control."

"Well, that's what we're here to do, Captain Fucking Obvious," Stevie tartly replied. She stood up and leaned me a helping hand, so I could get to my feet. I didn't want to talk about this anymore. I just wanted to go back to the cabin and sleep and deal with all this shit tomorrow. It felt like my head was going to explode.

"We still need to finish our discussion." Would Randall ever shut up about this fucking treaty?

"I think Ryan needs rest after what just happened," Jax answered, looking over and giving me a kind smile. I nodded in return. I felt like Jax could see I was at my limit for the day.

"You do not tell her what she does and does not need, dog," Kai roared, and before another fight broke out I quickly intervened.

"Look, guys—I have had a hell of day and night. If you have to talk, fine, but I'm going home. I'm wiped out." With that said, I started walking to the door, only to be stopped when Kai suddenly appeared in front of me. I screamed. What I can say? I startle easily.

"Forgive me, mi amor. I did not mean to scare you," he said, placing a hand on my shoulder. His touch sent shivers down my spine. In this moment, I would kill to have had his hand or mouth somewhere else. *What the fuck is wrong with me?* I can't do this with him anymore. He's a real person and not just part of my imagination. A part of me felt so betrayed that he lied to me. How would he have told me he was real, though—would I have believed him?

"Take your hands off her. We will discuss this tomorrow. My sister is tired, and we will be taking her home now," Stevie announced to the whole room. Kai was gone in a flash. I looked over my shoulder to see him standing by the king. I guess being a vampire meant you were super-fast. They all started discussing when and where to meet tomorrow. I tuned out of their conversation, not wanting to worry myself with more details that would make my head spin. I started for the door again for like the tenth time tonight. When I felt a hand land on the small of my back, I knew who it was before I even saw him; my body reacted to his touch like a paper to a flame. I turned to face Kai.

"Hey, I'm sorry if I got you in trouble."

"I'm fine, mi amor. I'm more worried about you."

"I'm fine; I've just got a lot going on in my head at the moment."

"I would love to try and help you figure out some of those things," he murmured.

"I need my sister and cousins to help me figure this power thing out, and I need you to tell me how you can get into my dreams." I really wished he could be the one to help me sort out this whole power thing, but at the moment I felt like I couldn't trust him. He lied to me. He was real this whole time and never told me. The things we did together in my dreams…God I feel like such a fucking fool. I was also so ashamed of myself. I behaved like a hussy in my dreams. I mean, my first time having sex in my dreams was with Kai.

"You would be surprised how much I would be able to help you with your power."

"What do you…" Jax, who stood just off to the side of me, interrupted before I could finish my sentence. He had a strange look on his face.

"We will meet again, Ryan. I'm sorry we couldn't talk more, but we will get another chance soon."

"Um...that's okay, and it was nice to meet you to Jax," I said with a forced smile.

"Tyler and I will come by the cabin in the morning to discuss some matters with you and your family." Just as he finished speaking, Kai pulled me in front of him and gripped my hips with both hands. I gasped at the contact, and he rested his chin on my head. Jax was growling like an angry dog. I knew what Kai was doing...he was telling Jackson that I was his and to back off. I wasn't his or anyone's, and I was about to tell him that, but he spoke first.

"If you plan on going past in the morning, I think I might make a point to join you all as well. I'm sure Ryan doesn't mind, do you, love?"

"Umm...no, you can come." Oh fuck, I just said that out loud. "I mean come to the cabin." I could feel the blush creeping up to my cheeks. I hung my head down in shame when I felt Kai shift and wrap one arm around my stomach, with the other lifting my head. He then whispered in my ear.

"Never look down, mi amor. Your eyes are far too beautiful to be hidden."

I blushed harder at that compliment. When he said stuff like this, it made me so confused. He lied to me, but then he could say a few words and I was eating out of the palm of his hand. Jax stepped forward and spoke through clenched teeth.

"There is no need for you to attend, enforcer...these matters do not concern you."

"Let's not start another pissing contest over my cousin's affections, okay, dickheads? Now get the fuck off her, Melakai, so we can go home." Chase looked disgusted, seeing how Kai was holding me.

Reluctantly, Kai let me go. I somehow knew it pained him to do so. I'll admit, it pained me as well. When he held me in my dreams, I felt safe and protected. I needed time to think. If he was real, then did that mean Nico was real too?

"How do you do it?" I asked Kai.

"Do what, mi amor?"

"How do you come to be in my dreams?"

"Ahhhh, Melakai, please do tell her how you acquired your gifts," Jax sneered at Kai.

"That is a story for another time, mi amor." Kai had a distant look in his eyes as he replied, like he was lost in a dark memory.

"Come, Ryan, let's get you home," Alex said, putting his arm around my shoulders and pulling me to him. With a final look at Kai, I let Alex lead me out of the office.

Chapter Twelve

We finally arrived at the cabin. I was too exhausted to worry about answers for my questions. I decided to get a good night's rest and drill the others in the morning. With a final bid good-night to my sister and cousins, I retired to my room.

After a quick shower, I slipped into a pair of sleep shorts and an old T-shirt. I climb into bed with a heavy feeling on my chest. When I wake up tomorrow, more shit in my life was going to change. I decided right there, in that moment, that I was not going to throw myself a pity party any longer. I was free from my mother and her abuse. I may not have gotten to see my father before he passed, but none of that would hold me back any longer. I was stronger than that.

Come tomorrow, I would take whatever came at me and demand the answers I needed to make sense of my life. I hated not having control of things in my life. I lived too long with no control, and I would never, never have that taken from me again.

I was a grown-ass woman now, not some meek kid that could be bullied or hurt. I turned on my side to try and get some sleep and my eyes landed on the letter my dad wrote me, still sitting on the nightstand. I wasn't ready to read that yet, so I did

what any grown women would do: I rolled back over and went to sleep.

I awoke to the feeling of the warm sun on my face. I smiled to myself. I was never allowed to sleep in. Mother forbade it; she would tell me weird stories about strange things, and I would have to repeat them to her, so she knew I was listening. The only reprieve I got from her was when I was at school or she was drunk and passed out. Refusing to let my thoughts consume me, I climb out of bed, stretching my arms high above my head. After finally being satisfied with my stretch, I made my way to the bathroom to quickly brush my teeth and wash my face. I wanted to meet the others for a nice quiet chat and get some answers, but that was not how it happened.

After exiting my room and making my way down the hall to the kitchen, I stopped dead in my tracks at seeing Tyler leaning against the front door, a smirk on his face.

"What the fuck is funny? And why the hell are you here?" I snapped putting my hands on my hips.

"I guess I'm not the only one standing up this morning," he said, wiggling his brows. I tilted my head to the side, not under-standing what he meant. Then I heard a cough and looked to see the others at the dining table.

"You might want to put a sweater on, Sissy. You seem a bit cold, if you know what I mean!" It hit me then what Tyler was laughing at: my fucking nipples were on high alert. I forgot to put a bra on before I left my room.

I quickly covered my chest and pinned Tyler with a dirty look and turned to go and change, when I heard him yell after me.

"I do love the little piggy sleep shorts you're wearing too, though, princess!" I groaned, could this morning get any worse? I wanted to slap that smug bastard Tyler.

I heard a growl come from the kitchen that I could only assume it was Jax trying to tell Tyler to shut his fat mouth. After quickly getting changed into a pair of skinny jeans, Ugg boots and a long-sleeved V-neck shirt—with a bra on this time—I left my room to re-join the others. Once in the kitchen, I made myself a quick cup of coffee and joined Chase at the table.

"Nice of you to join us, squirt," Alex quipped.

"Your mouth is as annoying as your face, Alex, so please shut it, would you?" I said with a devilish smile.

"Well, I guess you're still not a morning person, then, eh, Sissy?" Stevie remarked with a snicker.

"Guess not, Sissy. Anyway, I want answers, and you are all going to give them to me. But first—Jackson, why are you here?" I saw a look of hurt flash past his eyes before he regained himself.

"I'm here to help you, Miss Knox, and to also discuss the treaty."

"Okay, no offense, but I don't give a shit about some treaty. I just want to know what the fuck I am and if I can give these 'gifts' back. I don't want and never asked for them. I just started to get my life back on track, and now all this shit comes out. I mean, can a chick catch a break?" I was flinging my arms in the air like a mad woman, but I didn't care. I just wanted them to understand that I didn't want any of this. They may like what they are, but I don't—not after last night, anyway.

"The day-walking leech is here, Alpha," Tyler sneered. Jackson just growled.

He didn't knock before entering; he just walked in like he owned the damn cabin. He nodded to the others and smiled at me. With a huff, I stood and shouted at no one in particular.

"Let's just invite the whole fucking neighborhood over, shall we? I mean, it's only Ryan who is the odd one out and doesn't know shit from dick, right? I stood by and listened while you all talked shit last night about shit I don't even know about, and now you want to do it again before I can get any answers! Hell to the mother-fucking-no!"

They all looked at me like I had just grown another head. I was pissed. Jax, Tyler, and now Kai are here? How am I ever going to get any answers, if all they wanted to do was talk about some fucking treaty?

"You a bit hungry, squirt? There's bacon and eggs in the microwave. You were never pretty in the mornings or when you're hungry," Chase said gently. I deflated a bit. He was right. I was a bitch in the mornings, and I was even worse when I was hungry.

"Only you know the way to my heart, cousin." I gave Chase a wink as I made my way to the microwave. Once I got my plate and sat back down at the table, I plopped a bit of bacon into my mouth and moaned—it was so good.

"I feel like I'm watching food porn" Alex joked while making a funny look with his face. With my mouth full of eggs, I replied.

"What can I say, food turns me on, baaabbbyyy." I heard Kai's sharp intake of breath and Jackson growl as soon as I finished speaking.

"Ryan, don't be a goddamn pig, we have guests!" Stevie's a party pooper. After swallowing my mouthful, I turned to my sister and tartly snapped back.

"Well, since my outburst, no one has even made a noise, so I forgot they were here, and it's not like we only just met. One stalks me in my dreams, the other follows me into the woods, and that one"—I said nodding my head in Tyler's direction—"just checked out my rack, so we may as well be besties, if you ask me."

Everyone laughed at that comment, and now with the mood lighter, Kai came and took the seat next to me. Tyler took the seat next to his alpha, on the other side of the table. I don't know why I was feeling nervous, but I started twisting my hands in my lap, waiting for someone to break the silence. My food was long forgotten now. Suddenly, I felt Kai's hand on mine, stopping them from fidgeting. I looked up and he gave me a reassuring smile, like everything was going to be okay. I don't know why, but that small gesture made me feel reassured.

"Okay, Ryan, we owe you that much. What would you like to know, squirt?" Alex asked, while leaning his elbows on the table.

"How am I like this? Like, how did I get this power or gift or whatever you call it? Why did you all freak out when I had that dream, in the car ride up here?" Kai gave my hand another reassuring squeeze. I felt better just with him touching me, like he would protect me from all the bad in the world. I was still pissed that he lied to me, but right now I needed his support while I dealt with this conversation.

Stevie cleared her throat and leaned forward to rest her forearms on the table.

"I don't know how else to say this, so I'm just going to say what I think, okay? All the fairy tales about witches, vampires, werewolves, fae, and so on are true. Our grandfather was the one that founded the treaty with Randall Cane and Jackson's father, to keep peace among the races. You're a born witch from the Knox coven, descendent of Marcus Knox, who was the leader and founder of the Alaskan coven."

"Okay, but why did you freak out, about the dream?"

"Because, we knew then that Melakai was coming for you" I was shocked at Stevie's reply. I didn't dare look to Kai; I wanted to hear my sister's reasons.

"What do you mean, coming for me, Stevie?"

"As you know, Melakai has certain gifts. We learned long ago that when he enters a mind, he can persuade a person to do his bidding, or the King's."

"Okay, I'll process that later. So I'm a witch, you're a witch, Alex and Chase are warlocks. Jax and Tyler are werewolves, and Kai and Randall are vampires. Who the fuck are the fae? I haven't heard any stories about them."

A look of pain passed over Jackson's face. He shook his head as if to clear his mind of the thoughts he was having. My heart ached for him, as the pain was so clearly written on his face. I could tell from that look he hated the fae. He spoke with such malice and hatred in his tone when he answered my question.

"The fae are vile creatures that prey on the weak and care for no one but their own kind. They are cruel, heartless beings and need to stay on their side of the veil. If they dare to step foot this side again, my pack will stop at nothing to eradicate their kind from this earth."

I felt like there was a big part of this story that I was missing. I don't know how, but I knew everyone was keeping something from me.

"Why do I feel like you all are being very cagey and not telling me the full story? I want to know all of it. Don't lie to me, please—you owe me that much, Stevie," I said, pinning my sister with a stern look. Stevie wasn't the one who answered my question, though.

"We have our suspicion that the fae are the ones who

murdered your father, Ryan." Wait a fucking minute! I thought my dad died from a sudden illness. "We have no proof, as of yet, but when we examined your father's body, there was a strong stench of magic on him. Every magic user leaves a trail. Witches have a certain scent, and once you have that scent, you will be able to tell who that scent belongs to. The one on your father was not from any witch. The only person or persons that could leave that scent are the fae," Alex said with a look of remorse on his face, like he never wanted to burden me with that secret.

I didn't know what to say. I felt so much guilt for my sister and my dad. I wasn't there when he passed, as I was so mad at him for leaving me with Mom. I should have been there for my sister, but I was too selfish and wouldn't listen to Stevie when she said she needed me to be there the day that he was buried. She never told me Dad was murdered.

She let me think he died of illness. I was angry all over again that she lied to me, but I needed to put my feelings aside for now and be there for my sister.

"Stevie, I am so, so sorry. I wasn't there for you when you needed me. I was so selfish." I hung my head in shame, knowing my sister had to deal with our father's funeral and burial on her own.

She shook her head and leaned over the table, her hand extended to me. I pried one of my hands from Kai's and grabbed my sister's. She looked at me with sadness in her hazel eyes.

"I forgive you, Ry. You had no idea what had happened, and I couldn't tell you all of this over the phone. We didn't want to tell you any of this at home, as we had a feeling they were still watching the house. That's why we left so soon after you arrived. We needed to get here and alert the coven and the pack, as well as Randall. If the fae are waging a war, we will need all the help we can get."

"I will help you all in any way I can. I will not let them get away with hurting our dad, Stevie—I swear."

"If what you say is true, why would the fae return now after so many decades of peace, and why only target your father?" Kai asked no one in particular. He seemed like he didn't believe that the fae were to blame, and that made me suspicious. Why is Kai defending these people, when he just heard that they killed my father?

"We have no idea. That's why we came here to seek answers we could not get at home, and to train Ryan. We fear that they now know of her existence and will come after both her and Stevie," Chase said, looking Kai directly in the eye, almost like he was challenging him.

"We must all prepare our people. The coven will want revenge for their king being killed at the hands of the fae. As their queen, I must honor their wishes." Stevie was pinning me with a look that implored me to understand what she was saying.

"You mean you want to *kill* the person that killed our father?" I couldn't murder someone in cold blood! We had a justice system for a reason.

She just nodded. I couldn't believe what the hell she was saying.

"You can't just go around fucking killing people Stevie, that's wrong—it's murder," I said, in shock.

"I can and I must— blood must have blood. That is our way, sister, and you will soon learn that." She snapped, anger lacing her words. What the hell is wrong with my sister?

"You are not the only coven queen now, Stevie," Jax retorted.

"I am the oldest, therefore the role is mine, not my sister's," she snapped back at him.

"That may be the case, but she can challenge you to a duel for the crown, can she not?" Jax asked.

I felt all eyes on me in that moment. I didn't know how to answer that, so I said the first thing that came to my mind.

"Let's talk about my dreams and how Kai is in them," I said, looking to anyone for answers before my eyes finally settled on Kai. With a sigh, he answered my question.

"Because of my gifts."

"What kind of gifts?" I asked.

"The kind of gifts that let me enter people's minds. I can alter their moods and emotions, if need be. I am the king's secret weapon." Well, not so secret anymore, dumbass.

"So that's why you were there last night? To get my sister and Jax to agree to change this treaty thing?" I heard the others gasp. Were my feelings for Kai real? Or were they part of his emotion control power? Jax stood up, leaning on the table, with a glare on his face. He was growling, and his eyes were changing color. They weren't chocolate brown anymore—they were yellow. Holy shit, I think Jax might be changing into a wolf right in front of me.

"You son of a bitch. She's right, isn't she? That fucker was trying to con us by using your *gifts* to get us to agree!" he roared. Tyler put a hand on Jackson's shoulder to calm him, but he just shook it off. Kai stood and leaned over the table so he and Jackson were nearly nose to nose.

"I have to follow orders and what my king wants, whether I think it's wrong or not. I must do as he asks." Okay, that's a bit weird. So Kai didn't like doing what Randall wanted all the time? That's good to know.

"Bullshit, Melakai. The enforcer is back in full swing now, ladies and gentlemen. You would have tried to kill us last night if we didn't agree, wouldn't you? That's why all those guards were nearby—in case all hell broke loose when you tried to take us out!" Jackson did have a good point with that.

"What is done cannot be un-done, Alpha, so there is no use worrying about what has not come to pass," Kai said, with annoyance thick in his tone.

Jackson couldn't take it anymore. He jumped across the table and grabbed Kai. It all happened so fast. I could see arms swinging left and right. Everyone was trying to break them up and shouting directions and threats. I grabbed hold of Kai's arm, but just as I gripped him by the elbow, he spun around and grabbed me by the throat. As soon as he realized it was me, he instantly dropped his hand, but it was too late. Jackson hadn't stopped. His fist connected with Kai's jaw, and I heard a crack. I was sure his jaw was broken from the force of Jax's punch.

I couldn't watch any longer. Kai was hunched over on one knee, a hand on his jaw, and was struggling to stand. I jumped in the middle, before they could continue to harm each other, and pinned each of them with glare of fury.

"Would you two learn to use your fucking words?" I shouted.

"That fucker deserved the punch he got for laying hands on you, squirt," Alex snapped. I looked over my shoulder to glare at him—he was not helping the situation.

"Not helping, Alex." I then retuned my focus to the two brooding males. "Both of you need to cool off and come back when you can apologize to each other, okay?"

With a reluctant nod from each of them, they left the cabin, letting us know they would be back later to discuss the treaty, again.

Chapter Thirteen

After Jax, Tyler and Kai left, Stevie and I told the boys we were going to go for a walk to catch up. They feigned hurt feelings, but truth was, they didn't care, and they wanted to watch some game that was on TV. Boys will be boys.

Stevie and I walked at a moderate pace through the woods, down a well-warn path that clearly had been used by animals and humans.

"Dad used to bring me up here all the time as a kid. I loved coming here—it always meant I could stop hiding who I was and be free. I couldn't do that back home." Stevie spoke with a faraway look in her eyes, like she was reliving a happy memory.

"Why didn't you and Dad just move here then?"

"He would never move a country away from you, Ry—even if it did feel that way to you growing up. We tried to come for you, Ry, so many times. But Mom got tired of our pleading and said if Dad came by again and tried to take you from her, she would expose what we were to the humans. Humans can never know we exist, Ry. They can't handle what they cannot control. They would exterminate us. That is why the treaty is so important—it keeps all the supes in the world in line."

"I never knew you tried to come for me. I just assumed Dad didn't want me. Mom always said Dad only wanted you. I guess I just believed her; I gave up waiting for him to come save me, Stevie. I know I shouldn't have, but I did."

"I never knew how hard it was for you until the first time you managed to get a hold of me and we finally saw each other after so many years. That's when I got a glimpse of how bad it was. I saw the bruises, Ryan, no matter how hard you tried to hide them, Sissy. I am so truly sorry, from the bottom of my heart, that I couldn't get you out. I was scared and weak, but I swear I will never fail you again, my sister. I am not scared or weak anymore."

I knew she was telling me the truth. I could hear the conviction in her voice. I knew, no matter what life threw at us, we would always stick together and fight for each other. We were two halves, but together we were whole.

"I know, Stevie, and you don't need to be sorry. It wasn't your fault. We were children. We didn't know any better." I gave her a playful bump with my hip to lighten the mood, which made her laugh. I was glad; I hated seeing her so sad.

"So anyway, enough sad shit. What's the deal with you and Melakai? I know Jackson Marshall is into you, as well. I can see the way they both look at you." I shook my head at her —she was so wrong.

"I don't know. Jax is nice and very handsome, but I don't know what to think about him, really. It's so confusing. Melakai, on the other hand, the day we came here, and I had that dream, I didn't even know who he was. I didn't know he was real. Now I'm more confused, because I can't tell if my feelings for him are real or are they part of his control over people's emotions."

"I get what you are saying, I do, but Jackson would be the better choice, if you ask me. Melakai seems so doom and gloom all the time. Would the guy's face break if he smiled? As for the emotion control...I have no idea, Ry. That is something you will have to ask him."

"Don't be mean. I don't want to jump into anything; I have way too much going on as it is, and a guy would just make things ten times worse." Changing the subject, I asked. "Why Alaska though Stevie?"

"Because this is where, dad was born." That was news to me. I thought dad was born in New Zealand, like us.

"I didn't know that. I guess it makes sense now why we are here. Why did dad leave?"

"He was sent on an overseas trip or something like that, some witches were going rogue in New Zealand and dad had to clean up the mess. While he was in New Zealand, he met mom. I guess he decided she was worth giving up his place here, to be with her."

"Were our grandparents okay with that?"

"I don't know to be honest. Dad never talked about his parents much." Oh, that's strange.

"Are they still here, in Alaska?" Stevie had a look on her face that I couldn't read.

"I don't actually know, I have never met them. I assumed they died because I have never seen them at the coven. Dad would always change the subject if I asked about them." Why would dad do that? What was he hiding?

We chatted about more mundane things as we walked through the woods, finding our way back to the cabin as dusk was approaching. We needed to be ready for the wolves and vampires when they came to discuss the treaty—and I now understood why it was so important.

Chapter Fourteen

When we arrived back at the cabin, the boys had dinner ready, so we quickly ate and then I headed to my room to have a shower before everyone arrived. Stepping back into my room with a towel wrapped around my hair and another around my body, I stopped dead in my tracks when I saw a man sitting on my bed.

He had blond hair that fell to his shoulders, blue eyes like the ocean, and a strong, tall frame. His shirt wrapped perfectly around his large arms. He was hot! He stood with his hands held up, as if surrendering. I don't know why I didn't scream for the others to help, but I felt a sense of calm wash over me, so I stood rooted to the floor.

"I do not mean to frighten you, Ryan. I am here because I need help, and you are the only one I believe can help me. Will you hear me out, please?" I couldn't speak, so I just nodded. He took three steps closer to me. There was only a foot of distance between us. His scent hit me hard—he smelled of wild flowers and trees. I loved wildflowers. He chuckled, as if he knew what his close proximity was doing to me. What the hell is wrong with me? I seem to be getting turned on by every damn guy, I need to get my shit together.

"My name is Simon. My people are being framed by one the clans, who are a part of your treaty. My people had nothing to do with the death of your father."

Holy fuck, he was fae.

"You're a fae, aren't you?" I asked him. He nodded. "I don't know why you are here, asking me to believe you. I don't even know you, and from what I understand, it's pretty obvious who killed my father."

"I had nothing to gain from your father's death. He was a fair ruler and a good king, but more than that, he was a good man, Ryan." He spoke as if he knew my father.

"Did you know my father?"

"Yes I did. I helped your grandfather gather the intel he needed to create the treaty, so we could all live in peace, and my people would stop being hunted. Many lives were lost in the last war between all the supernatural kinds."

"So, you knew my grandfather as well then?"

"Yes."

"Why are you telling me this and not my sister? I don't know much about all this supernatural stuff. I just found out I was a witch yesterday."

"Ah, but you are so much more than just a witch, Ryan. Ask your precious vampire Melakai. He knows the truth." There was anger behind his words, and I couldn't imagine why.

"What do you mean?" And how does he know about Kai?

"I'm afraid our time is up. Please heed my words. My people are not to blame." I could hear it in his voice—he was telling the truth, and that confused me even more. "I will find you again, Ryan."

He turned and just vanished. I had no time to ponder what the fuck had just happened, because my bedroom door flew open, and Jax and Melakai barged in with feral looks on their faces. Melakai came to me and put his hands on my shoulders, leaning in to sniff me. He bloody sniffed me!

"What the hell do you both think you are doing in here?" I snapped, yanking my body out of his hands, just now noticing that I was half naked. I gripped my towel tighter.

"Who was in here with you Ryan?" Jax asked, with an agitated look on his face. I don't know why I lied, but I knew if I told them what just happened and who was in my room, all hell would break loose.

"No one was in here." They both gave me a look that said I was full of shit.

"I can smell someone else was in here, Ryan. I can't place the scent, but it is familiar to me. I know you weren't alone," Jackson said, taking a step forward.

"So, you're calling me a liar then?"

"I can tell when you lie, love," Jax replied with narrowed eyes.

"I heard you talking to someone, tell me who it was," Kai demanded.

"One—don't fucking tell me what to do, and two, get the fuck out, both of you—NOW!" I shouted. How dare they fucking barge in here.

With one last look at me, they both turned and left my room. I finally released the breath I didn't realize I was holding, and quickly got changed into some leggings and a long-sleeved shirt. On my way out, I grabbed my Ugg boots and slipped them on. I felt like we needed to hold off on blaming the fae. I didn't understand why I trusted what Simon said about his people not having anything to do with my father's death, but I did.

Upon arriving in the kitchen, I saw that everyone was seated, waiting for me to join them. I saw a space between Alex and Melakai, but after what had just transpired in my room, I did not want to be anywhere near Melakai. I walked over to the table and nudged Alex over so I could sit between him and Chase. Alex looked confused, assuming I would be more than pleased to sit next to Kai. Yeah, not right now buddy—he's on my shit list.

Once seated between my two cousins, I addressed the group.

"Sorry for keeping you all waiting. I was rudely interrupted by two overbearing jackasses, which delayed me." I delivered this with a fake hostess smile. Chase was giggling beside me, and Alex coughed to mask his laughter.

Stevie pinned us all with a disapproving look that had us sitting up straight and wiping the smiles off our faces.

"Don't worry about it, Ry. We all just sat down," Stevie said. "Now that we are all here, let's discuss the treaty, shall we? Ry, just to fill you in a bit, every time a new leader is appointed, the treaty needs to be re-signed, so that all parties are up to date with what is expected of each coven, pack,vampires and fae."

"Do all the vampires, packs, covens and fae all over the world have to obey this treaty?" I asked.

"Yes, they do, as we are the head of all of our kind. If any witches step out of line and judgment must be passed, they are brought here to stand trial before our coven elders and king, while now it's queen. Same as for the wolves and the vampires, I don't know how the fae do things. They do have an elder council like the rest of us though." Stevie answered. I nodded my understanding. I guess since everyone hated the fae at the moment, they wouldn't be signing the new treaty.

"Okay. Now that Miss Knox is up to speed, may we continue?" Randall Cane asked.

"Yes, why don't you start, Randall, and tell us all why you want to change the treaty and what your reasons for the changes are?" my sister asked.

"I want the fae realm completely sealed so that they may never enter this realm. In order to do that, I need the witches to try seal it and the pack sign off on it," Randall said, like we were all supposed to agree with him.

"If we do that, Farrarie will die. You know it needs to be stabilized by Earth," Alex said, with a look of shock on his face, as if he couldn't believe Randall had just said what he did.

"I am well aware of that, Mr. Knox, but I do not care. Their kind has done enough damage, don't you think? And if what Melakai has told me is true, I would think you would be open to this idea, given what they did to your uncle." It was clear what Randall wanted.

"That cannot happen. You will kill innocent fae women and children. We cannot condemn a whole race for the actions of a few. That's inhumane!" Chase bellowed, pounding his fist on the table.

"WE ARE NOT HUMAN, BOY!" the king shouted, rising to his feet.

"Watch your tone and how you speak to my cousin, king," I sneered, coming to Chase's defense. How dare he yell at my cousin, the old prick! King or not, he would not speak to my cousin like that.

"You should not speak of matters you know nothing about, little witch. Be seen, not heard," he shot back.

I stood, fists balled at my sides, ready to give him a piece of my mind, when I felt Kai place his hand on my shoulder, as if to sit me down. The king had a smile on his face, like he thought Melakai could settle me. I shrugged his hand off my shoulder with a vicious twitch.

"Don't fucking touch me, douche bag. You're on my shit-list at the moment." A look of hurt passed over his face, but he quickly gathered himself and masked it. I pointed my finger at the smirking king. "Do not ever speak to me or my family like that again! I don't give two shits who the fuck you are. You don't know me or what the fuck I have been through - if I want to say something, I will."

My sister stood, fire blazing in her hazel eyes, but her anger wasn't directed at Randall. She was angry with me.

"Enough, Ryan, sit down! Cane does have a valid point. The fae have caused so many problems in the past, and given what had happened to our father, I would have thought you would have been more on board with this."

"Are you serious? You haven't heard a word Alex or Chase has said, have you? You would wipe out a whole race like the shit under your shoe, just to help you sleep better at night?" I snapped back at my sister.

"You know nothing, Ryan. I must do this for my coven. Blood must have blood, no matter the cost. If wiping them all out is the answer, then so be it! I am the queen of this fucking coven and I decide—not you! Do I make myself clear, sister?" There was so much anger in her voice, and her words hurt me more than I could say. I fought to keep the tears at bay. I climbed off the bench seat and headed for my room, when her words stopped me. "You do not get to walk away from me. I am your queen. You will answer me when I ask you a question. Do you understand me, Ryan?"

I peered over my shoulder, staring at my sister, tears running freely down my face. I saw Jax's eyes soften when he looked at me. Both Alex and Chase had looks of pity on their faces. Kai looked hurt—not for himself but, for me.

"If following a queen means killing innocent people just to please her desires and selfishness, then I want no part of that queen's coven. If you do this, Stevie, you are a monster! You are no better than her!" I spat those words at my sister like they were acid on my tongue. A look of hurt quickly morphed to anger on her face, and her eyes went blank for a moment before she regained control. She climbed off her chair and came toward me.

I turn to face her head-on, using the back of my hand to wipe the tears away. I was waiting for the verbal abuse, but that never happened. Instead, she slapped me right across the face. The force was so great, I lost my footing and fell to the floor. I touched my cheek, which was now stingy and pulsating. I look up at my sister with utter disbelief; the girl staring down at me wasn't my sister. The person looking at me was full of rage and disgust. If looks could kill, I would be dead.

"You will never speak to me, your queen, that way again, Ryan, do I make myself clear?" She looked so power hungry. I couldn't believe what she had just done, and what she was now saying to me. She promised me just hours ago that she would never let anyone hurt me again, and now she was the one doing it to me. A surge of anger shot through my veins, and I stood up to face my sister. I was done having people lie to me and hide things from me and treat me like I was nothing. I was not going to let another person hurt me ever again.

When we were face to face, so close that our noses were nearly touching, I heard Tyler say from his seat at the table, "Oh fuck, shit's about to get real now, boys."

I looked my sister directly in the eyes, and I couldn't see the loving, caring person anymore. I only saw a power-hungry girl, trying to prove she was woman enough to lead, even if it meant killing innocent people.

"I am not that weak child who you can use as a punching bag, like Mom did, Stevie. I will not let you do to me what she did. I will not stand by and allow another person to dictate my life. I don't give a fuck if you are some coven queen. You will never be my queen, sister, if you do this. I will never follow someone who murders innocents, sister or not." I brushed past her and headed to my room to pack my things. I couldn't stay under the same roof as a person who thought it was okay to treat me the way she just did.

Once in my room, I slammed my door shut and sat on the edge of my bed. I couldn't stop the sob that crept out. After everything I had been through in my life with my mom, the one person I thought who would understand my need for change and a new life was Stevie. I was so wrong. She was exactly like

Mom; she just hid her monster better. I saw the look she had in her eyes—it was the same look Mom had when she used to beat the devil out of me.

I didn't hear my door open over my sobs, and I jumped when I felt a hand on my shoulder. I could tell Jackson was upset about what had just happened, and I didn't want him feeling sorry for me. I was sick of being pitied by people.

"I know we don't really know each other well, but Stevie had no right to do and say what she did, Ryan. What she did was out of order."

"I don't know what I am going to do now. I cannot stand by and watch a whole race be destroyed because of my sister's rage, Jackson. That's not who I am. I will not follow a queen who is prepared to sacrifice the lives of innocent people just to satisfy her own blood lust. I'm not like her," I said though my tears.

He shushed me and started rubbing his hand up and down my back, trying to soothe me, in a bid to stop my crying.

"I know you are different from your sister. I can see it in your eyes. You have an innocence about you that is so captivating to see and very rare to find in our kinds. The world we live in is so different to the one you were raised in, Ryan. We answer death with death. That's all we know. We were never taught any different." His voice was so soft and smooth, and it made me feel calm. The tears slowly stopped falling. I pulled away to rest against the headboard, and Jackson sat at the bottom of the bed.

"Can't you all change the way you view things?" I asked, my throat scratchy from all the crying.

"I wish it was that simple, but so much has happened between the supernatural races, Ryan. The vamps, witches, and wolves came to an understanding many years ago that ensured peace to all our people. The fae have upset that balance. The fae king, Nicholas Stone, signed the same treaty as my father and Randall. Your father also signed that same treaty. The fae king agreed to the terms that were stated. The king and his people would remain in Farrarie and never step foot on Earth as long as we left the portal open, so that their world wouldn't die."

"Why did the first war start?"

"The fae killed my father." Oh my God, so that's why Jax hated the fae. They killed his dad and broke the treaty. That's why they were all so anxious to write a new one and cut the fae out.

"I'm so sorry, Jackson, I didn't know." I grabbed his hand and held it, giving it a squeeze.

"It's okay, Ryan." His words had no conviction in them. They were hollow.

"How many treaties have there been?"

"Two. The first was with my father, Randall, your grandfather, and the fae king. The second was signed by Randall, my father, your father, and the fae king. The one we are trying to discuss now will be the third."

"How come a new one was never signed when you became Alpha?"

"Because your father helped me protect my people from other supes, who wished to challenge me for my throne. It is my birthright to be alpha of my people. When the time came for me to sit on the throne, I had grown strong, and that was thanks to the aid of your father. He trained me and taught me how to be a good and fair king to my people. He put off the signing of the new treaty til he knew I understood what I was doing. When the time came, it was too late—he was gone. That's why Randall is pushing so hard now. Stevie and I are both new leaders, and we both must sign."

Holy shit, I never expected that. My dad was that kind of man. What he did for Jackson spoke volumes of the kind of a man he was. Instead of trying to kill Jackson and take over his pack to gain power, he helped him and kept putting off the signing of the treaty until Jackson was old enough and strong enough to rule on his own.

"I'm so glad my dad was there for you and helped you out, Jackson. I'm sorry that I pulled you away from the treaty meeting. I know you need to be out there, so you can go." I felt guilty for taking up so much of his time.

He cupped my chin and lifted my head so he could look me in the eyes.

"Never look down, Ryan. You are royalty and have every right to the throne as well. You can challenge your sister for the throne, you know, and rule your people in the way you see fit." His eyes held so much hope that I couldn't get any words out. He took that as his cue to lean in. Just as his lips were about to touch mine, a knock sounded at the door. Startled by the noise, I jerked back and tried to get my breathing under control. Shit, I was about to let Jackson kiss me!

My bedroom door opened to reveal Tyler.

"The meeting has hit a stalemate for now. We will continue the discussion tomorrow at the king's manor, so all parties can go over what has been said." Jax gave Tyler a nod and stood up to leave.

"I hope we will see you tomorrow, Ryan. Until then, please take care of yourself, and if you need anything, just call me." He handed me a card with his number on it. I thanked him and wished them both a good night.

Once they left, I settled down in bed and shut my eyes, thinking I would just have a minute's rest before packing my bag and leaving this place for good.

Chapter Sixteen

I must have fallen asleep, as when I awoke, I was in my dream woods again.

As soon as I realized where I was, I called out to him, knowing he wouldn't be far away.

"I know you're here Melakai—you may as well just come out!" I shouted, turning around in a circle until my eyes landed on the shirtless vampire. Yummy.

"You catch on fast, mi amor," he said, walking toward me.

"I'm a quick study, what can I say," I drawled, sarcasm thick in my tone. I didn't want to be here. I wanted to wake up so I could get my shit together and get the fuck out of the cabin and away from my sister.

"I am sorry if I upset you tonight. That was not my intention." I could hear the sincerity in his voice.

"Look, don't worry about it. It's just been a long day and night."

"Will you walk with me?" he asked, his hand extended toward me. I didn't have enough fight left in me to refuse, so I placed my much smaller hand in his and let him lead me through the woods. We walked a few minutes before he stopped us at the

lake and he sat down. He looked at me, asking me with his eyes if I would sit. With a loud exhale, I sat down reluctantly.

"Will you let me tell you a story, mi amor?" I could see he was torn on whether or not to tell me this story, so I nodded. I mean, curiosity did kill the cat.

"Many years ago, the supernatural races used to be at peace. Until one day a greedy king fell in love with a woman of a different race, who was of royal blood herself. She left her people to live with the king in his realm. They married soon after, and they spent many happy years together, so in love with one another. The king—slowly over time—became so obsessed with gaining power that he hurt many people and took many lives to get what he wanted. He wanted to rule all the races and be the king of all the supernatural kind. The queen couldn't stand by and let him continue to hurt others for his own selfish gain, so she tried to stop him.

"He saw her act as treachery and sentenced her to life as a slave. She was beaten, raped, and made to work as the king's personal handmaid. The queen was very powerful in her own right, but she could not access her full power because the king had a witch cast a spell to keep her weak; he worried that she would be the only one in his realm strong enough to kill him, so he took precautions to ensure that never happened.

"What the king did not expect was for her to fall pregnant to some warlock that was one of the many to defile her. The king could never sire children himself; he was sterile. He was enraged by the sight of her and the knowledge that she was carrying some other man's child within her womb. He locked her in the dungeon, planning that when she gave birth he would kill the child while she watched, as a punishment. The queen could not let that happen to her child. She saved what little magic she had left so she could portal the child out of the castle as soon as the child was born. She was almost starved to death *by the time the child came; the king was hoping that if she wasn't fed enough that the child would die in the womb, but that never happened. The queen gave birth to a healthy baby girl. She knew she didn't have long before the king came to kill the child, so she quickly teleported the child out of there, but she didn't have enough strength to take herself. She chose to save her child's life over her own. When the king came to collect the child, he was so angered at her defiance that he killed the queen with his bare hands.*

The king never found the child, no matter how long and far he searched. What he didn't know was that the queen had cloaked the child so that no vampire may ever find her or harm her. You see, that child would be one of the most powerful children to walk the earth; it was part witch and part fae—no one could ever match the child in strength or power. The only curse the child would bear from her mother was that she could never access the power herself, only her offspring.

Blinded by rage, the king unintentionally started a war by killing the queen. Her people wanted his blood for what he had done, and the king could not win a war against her people on his own. He needed the other supes to stand with him. He knew they would not stand by his side, for it was his own stupidity that started the war, so he needed to think fast.

And so he killed one of the leaders of another supernatural race and pinned it on the queen's people. He got what he wanted in the end—all the supes rallied to his aid. He told them that the queen's own people had killed her and tried to blame him because they wanted to start a war.

After the king had won the battle against the queen's people and banished them to their lands, he went in search of the child once again only to finally find the child and realize that the child had no powers of any kind. She was as human as they came, and the king went about his business, confident that she would live and die, as all weak humans did, not knowing that this human would pass on the power she inherited through her children.

And so it came to pass that the queen's daughter gave birth to twin girls, but only one child could receive the power of both fae and witch: the child with the purest heart, received those powers."

I had been listening carefully to his tale, making sure I had the details straight, and so after he finished I sat there quietly, trying to piece together the story. Then it suddenly hit me. I jumped to my feet.

"Wait—so you're telling me that my mother is the daughter of the fae queen, and my sister and I are half fae and half witch?" I screeched.

He stood and placed both his hands on my shoulders, almost like he was keeping me grounded for the bomb he was about to drop.

"No, mi amor, your sister is full witch. You are half fae and half witch. Only the child with the purest heart could wield the powers of both races."

Holy fuck.

"No. No, that can't be. My dad was a warlock, and my mom was human. I'm not who you think I am, and if what you say is true, what is the fae king to me?"

"Yes, in a way your mother was human, but only because her powers were inaccessible to her. The fae king is of no relation to you, as he was only king of the north and east at that time. The queen was the princess of the south and west. She would have been queen of fae realm had she not left to marry the king. During the Great War, her father died, so now Nicholas Stone rules the north, east, south, and west. They are all one kingdom now."

"Wait—who the fuck is the king, the one the queen married,

then?" I had a good idea who he was going to say, but needed him to confirm it.

"The Vampire King Randall Cane," he said dispassionately. How the fuck could the queen marry that asshole?

"Holy shit, he was the one that killed Jackson's dad, not the fae…" It was more a statement than a question, but he nodded anyway. "The fae didn't kill my father, did they? Randall Cane did, didn't he? He's still trying to take the leaders out so he can rule all the supernatural kind."

"I cannot be sure of that, but I do suspect it was him, and yes, he is still trying to take over, but he didn't account for Jackson surviving the war. He started trying to rule the wolves after the war had ended, but your father protected Jackson, and Jackson's people were loyal to him. They knew he would take the throne and responsibility that came with it when he was strong enough. By then it was too late."

"Why are you telling me this, Melakai?"

He had a look of regret on his face, like he was about to dump the world on my shoulders, and in a way he kind of was.

"Your sister and the king have decided to seal the fae realm, which means Farrarie will die, and if that happens, that means all the fae will die."

I knew the point of the story now—if the fae realm was closed, and if I am half fae, that would mean I would die along with them.

"I get what you are saying, but what the hell am I supposed to do about any of this? You saw what happened last night; my sister will never listen to me."

"You need to try, mi amor, for if they succeeded in doing what they plan, your people will die, as will you." He leaned down to look me in the eyes while placing his hands on my hips, and my body temperature skyrocketed. My body had a mind of its own whenever he touched me.

"They are not my people, okay? I will try to help them, but that does not mean I will ever accept being part fae, if it is true." With a nod of his head and a large exhale of air, he spoke.

"I can accept that and I thank you for helping"

There was one thing I couldn't quite get though, how the hell did he know all of this and how did he know so much. Was he a fae, no he couldn't be because he was a vampire an un-dead so to speak? I had to ask him, I needed to know but I had a sinking feeling I wasn't going to like his answer.

"How do you know all of this, Melakai?" I watched his face closely for the truth.

He tensed slightly and tried to cover it up as fast as he could, but it was too late—I had felt it.

"I knew the fae queen," he said, dropping his head in shame.

"Wait, so you were there when all of this happened?"

"Yes."

"Are you Randall Cane's son?"

"Yes and no." Vague much?

"Which is it, Melakai? And I want the goddamn truth," I said, pulling away from his grip so I could have a few feet of space between us. I couldn't think straight when he was so close, and he knew it too.

"I am his son through a blood oath, but not by blood."

"Explain, please." He sat back down on the grass and once again patted the spot next to him in invitation. I relented with a huff and dropped down beside him.

"When the fae queen first came to live with the king, I made sure I was the best and most trusted enforcer. I was assigned to escort the queen everywhere and guard her with my life always. I did this for many years, until the king banished her to be a slave, and even then I would look out for her. She was a kind and caring woman. She loved everyone and everything. It was just who she was. I thought the warlock that impregnated her had raped her like the others, so I ended his life. What I could never have foreseen was that the queen and the warlock had a bargain: she would bear him a child if he helped her open a portal back to Farrarie to her people, where she could get help. I killed the only hope she had for her freedom. I tried in every way I could to help the queen to escape, but all attempts proved futile.

Once the child was born, I tried to delay the king as long as I could to give the queen time to teleport her child out of the dungeon and into its new life. I never thought the king would kill the queen, and I was too late to save her. I made a vow in that moment to never let anything happen to the queen's child."

"So you knew this whole time where my mom was?"

"Yes."

"How?"

"The spell the queen cast was to cloak the child from any vampire that wished to harm her. I did not wish to harm her, therefore I was able to locate the child." His matter of fact responses were raising my ire.

"Why do you seem like this isn't a big deal? You knew where the fae queen's child was this whole time and never told the king? How do you know the king killed Jackson's father?" If he had helped the king commit these crimes, I would find a way to end him and the king both. I could never trust Melakai again if he had helped kill my father.

"I followed the king every night while the queen was locked up, to see what he was doing and if he would visit the witch that had blocked the queen's powers. I saw him lure Jackson's father away from his people on a false pretense of spies in his pack, swearing him to secrecy. That was how the king killed the pup's father. I told you I have no proof he was involved in your father's death; I only suspect that he did, because he's done it before."

I was trying so hard to keep up with what he was saying when a thought suddenly struck me.

"You saw, didn't you?" He tilted his head to the side, a look of confusion on his face.

"Saw what, mi amor?"

"What my mother did to me. You saw it all, didn't you?"

A look of pain, anger, and heartbreak crossed his face before he hung his head in shame. He didn't need to reply—his face and body language gave me all the answer I needed. I jumped to my feet and couldn't stop the words from pouring out of my mouth.

"You gutless, spineless, son of a bitch!" I screamed at him. He jumped to his feet and tried to grab me, but I side-stepped him and continued my rant. "You have the nerve to stand before me and claim to want to protect me from harm, when you let a monster abuse me for years, when you could have saved me from all of it. You just stood by and watched her beat me and starve me and tear me down to nothing. How do you look at yourself every day, knowing you could have saved a child from a lifetime of misery? You're a fucking coward!"

I slapped him so hard across the face that my hand developed a pulse. I couldn't stop screaming at him, calling him every name I could think of while pacing and swinging at him wildly. After a few minutes he finally had enough and grabbed both my arms and spun me around so my arms were locked behind my back and my back was to his chest. We were both breathing fast and hard. After he gained his composure, he spoke.

"I tried to help, Ryan, and I made it fucking worse okay, I confronted your mother while you were at school —you must have been eight or nine. I told her the truth of who and what she was. She didn't believe me at first, until I showed her my fangs and what I truly am. She screamed at me to leave and never come back, or she would kill you. She was mentally unstable. I couldn't trust that if I came to you and told you what you were, that you wouldn't tell her you had met me. I saw what happened that night when you came home from school, and I am so sorry,

Ryan, for my part in making matters worse, I truly am." That was the first time Kai had ever called me by my name.

I was still trying to calm myself after hearing what he had said. I knew which night he was talking about—that was the night everything changed for me and my mother. She threw me down the stairs, and I hit my head so hard that I needed stitches and had a concussion. It didn't end there. After getting home from the hospital, she used the belt on my ass until I passed out from the pain. Now I knew why she had done it: she hated me so much after finding out what I was that she was trying to beat the magic out of me. She was jealous of me.

"Get your hands off me now and let me go. I want to wake the fuck up now, and I want you to stay the hell away from me, Melakai Cane!" As I spat that last word out, I felt him flinch behind me, and I knew it was wrong to blame him for what my mother had done, but I didn't care. I was angry and hurt and even ashamed, and I wouldn't spend a minute longer with someone who watched my abuse and did not stop it.

He released my hands, and I spun around to look at him. His eyes betrayed his surface calmness; they had a storm brewing inside them. He finally gave up the staring contest and nodded.

He turned to leave, but stopped and looked over his shoulder and whispered, "I am so very sorry, mi amor; I wish I had done more. Just know that I was there, even if you do not remember." I had no idea what the hell that meant. I gave him a curt nod of my head and then everything went dark once more.

I woke the next morning feeling more exhausted than when I went to sleep. I was in no rush to leave my room this morning, knowing I would have to face my sister. That was a conversation I was more than happy to put off.

I dragged myself out of bed and hopped in the shower, hoping it would release some tension in my body. After showering, I towel-dried my hair and put on a pair of my most comfy sweats and paired them with a plain black singlet, I threw a red and black checkered flannel shirt over the top. After changing, I went back into the bathroom to finish doing my hair, and when I looked at the mirror, I was shocked by the person I saw.

My eyes seemed more greenish-yellow, and my hair was shinier and richer in color. I looked more a woman than a girl. The changes wouldn't be noticeable to anyone other than myself, but I felt a surge of confidence shoot through me, along with an ember of hope that maybe some man might be able to love me for me someday. I quickly pushed those thoughts aside, because I had enough to worry about without adding man problems.

I ran a brush through my hair and tied it into a high ponytail. I needed to think about how I was going to tell the others what I had learned without making myself look like a crazy person. Easier said than done, if you ask me. Knowing I couldn't hole up in my room forever I pushed myself off my bed with a sigh and went to search for the others.

The boys were kicked back on the couches in the living room, watching TV. I bid them a cool greeting and went to the kitchen to find my sister. She was at the bench, staring out the window. I cleared my throat to get her attention. She snapped her head my way, looking at me with eyes that I didn't recognize—it was like the light had been sucked out of her. She shook her head, and then her eyes changed from the dark green I had just seen back to their normal hazel-green color. I couldn't explain it, but something was not right with my sister.

"Morning," I said.

"Hi," was her frosty response. Wow, she thought she had a right to be pissed at me? Other way around, Stevie—you fucked up, not me.

"Look, I need to talk you about something," I said while taking a seat on one of the bench chairs.

"Unless it's an apology, I'm good, thanks."

"Are you fucking kidding me right now?" I couldn't believe this. She wants me to say sorry after she hit me? Bitch much? I was stunned.

"No, I am not. The way you behaved last night, and the way you spoke to me in front of the other leaders, is unacceptable Ryan. If you want to talk, apologize first, then we can work something out from there." I snorted, and she narrowed her eyes at me.

"You may think I am in the wrong here, but I am not, Stevie. You need to hear what I have to say, or it will be on your head when the treaty goes to shit," I said, my fury rising.

"The treaty is none of your concern sister; I signed it this morning when Randall came by."

Holy shit, she just sealed my death warrant and the whole of Farrarie with what she has done. I walked right up to my sister so we were eye to eye; she needed to see the truth in my eyes.

"You stupid fool; you have no idea what the fuck you have done. You are a murderer, Stevie! The blood of every fae will be on your hands, and *so will mine.*" She just stared at me with a blank look on her face; I had nothing left to say to her. She wouldn't listen to anyone but herself; she thought what she was doing was right. I pushed passed her and went back to my room to think of a new plan, one that involved saving my life and the fae realm.

I went to sit on the day bed right by the window; it was such a beautiful sight to see the snow falling and watch the ground be blanketed with white. The sun was out, and there was a slight breeze outside. It was a beautiful day. It helped raise my spirits a bit. Just as I leaned back on the pillows and closed my eyes, there was a knock at my door. Not bothering to open my eyes I told whoever it was to come in.

"Hey, squirt, we need to talk to you." I opened my eyes immediately to see both my cousins standing in the doorway; I waved them over and told them to have a seat. Chase closed the door and sat on the edge of the bed while Alex leaned on the wall beside the window.

"What's up, guys?" I asked, curious as to what they had to say.

"About last night..." Alex began but I cut him off.

"Don't cry over spilled milk, Alex. I'm a big girl, and I get it that you guys can't stand against her because she's your leader. It's fine. I don't blame you or have any ill feelings toward either of use for it," I said with a slight smile on my lips, hoping to ease their guilt.

Alex shook his head. "We do not condone what Stevie did to you, Ryan, nor do we agree with her decision to sign the treaty and seal the fae world from ours. A whole race cannot be accountable for the actions of a few."

"So what does this mean?"

"It means, squirt, we want to try stop her, and something you said caught our attention earlier," Chase answered.

"What did I say?"

"That your blood would be on her hands if she signed the treaty. What did you mean by that?" Alex asked with a quirk of his brow. You could always count on Alex to listen to every word someone said.

"It means that if she seals the portal to Farrarie off, she will kill all the fae, me included."

They both exchanged a look of worry and confusion, but Chase was the one who spoke first.

"Ryan, if you're thinking of taking your own life to prove a point, there are other ways! We can help you through this." He looked so broken in that moment, like he wanted to lock me away where no one could harm me and I couldn't harm myself. An inappropriate giggle burbled out of me before I could stop it; it was a nervous habit.

"This isn't fucking funny, Ryan. We're serious," Alex said, annoyance thick in his tone; I stopped laughing and answered him.

"I am not going to harm myself in any way, I promise you that. I have to tell you both something, but you may want to take a seat; it's a long-ass story." They both nodded and made themselves comfortable. "Where's Stevie?"

"She went out to see if she could get Jackson to sign the

treaty. He said he needed time to think about it, which I guess is a good thing," Chase said.

"Well, listen up." I recounted Melakai's story about the vampire king and fae queen to them. Their expressions morphed from awe to confusion, then hatred and anger. I could relate to how they were feeling, but rather than getting heated and being irrational, we needed to come up with a plan—and fast. If I know my sister like I think I do, she will be trying to get this plan done by whatever means necessary.

Alex leaned forward, placing his forearms on his thighs and asked, "Wait, so if the queen had a kid, and then that kid had twin girls, we need to find them and protect them from the king?"

"If he finds the child that inherited both witch and fae powers, we are all royally fucked," Chase said, exasperated.

I stared at them both, astonished at their failure to connect the dots. "Well, boys, we have already found the girls."

"Where are they, Ryan? We need to go get them now!" Alex demanded while pacing the floor. And to think Alex was the brainy kid of the family.

"One is out there, and the other is in here," I told them, Okay, maybe I was enjoying having the upper hand on Alex for once.

"What the fuck does that mean, Ryan? Stop being cryptic and spit it out. Their lives are in danger!" Alex retorted. I let out a loud huff of air before standing and looking at them both.

"Stevie is the first born twin, and I am the second born!"

"Dear God," Chase said, placing his hand over his mouth.

"I fucking know that, Ryan, but where—" Chase cut Alex off with a growl.

"You are not listening, dipshit; Stevie and Ryan are the granddaughters of the fae queen. Stevie isn't the one with both fae and witch power—*Ryan is.*" Chase turned to look at me, and he looked scared, but not for himself. Alex stopped pacing and stared at me in disbelief.

"Holy fuck, Ryan. This isn't good at all. If they seal the fae realm off, you'll die?" Alex asked

"Yes, Alex, if she goes through with this, I will die. We need to figure this out fast, but I don't know how to stop this. Stevie has gone so power hungry that I don't even recognize her," I said.

"I can agree that the power has gone to her head a bit," Chase said, shaking his head.

"We need to try talk to her tonight, and if she won't listen, then we're on our own," Alex stated grimly.

We all agreed to talk to her tonight at dinner. We all hoped she would see reason and stop this madness, but a part of me knew my sister wouldn't listen. The look in her eyes told me enough this morning.

After the boys had left my room, I went through my bag and pulled out my favorite book, *Night Flame,* by Catherine Hart. I sat back in my chair by the window, prepared to spend the rest of the afternoon reading, when a shiver ran down my spine. I jumped out of my seat and spun around to see a pair of yellow eyes glowing in the corner of the room. As those eyes drew closer to me, I realized that it was Simon, the fae that came to warn me the other day.

"Hi," I said, keeping my voice low so the others wouldn't hear.

"Hello, Ryan, may I speak with you, please?"

"Sure, hang on one sec, okay?" I dashed over to the other side of the bed and grabbed my iPod so I could plug it in to the speaker. With that going, if anyone went past my room, they wouldn't hear us talking. As I set the iPod to play, the song that started was one of my favorites, Frankie J's song, "Obsession."

"Clever you are, my dear," Simon said as I walked back to take my seat. I waved to the bed so that he could sit, and he did. I looked at him, thinking that he reminded me of someone, just the way he moved and how he looked at me, but I just couldn't think who it was.

"What can I do for you, Simon?"

"I have been keeping an eye on things here in this realm regarding the treaty. I see your sister is still out for blood, as is the vampire king."

"Look, I've tried to talk to her but she won't listen. My cousins and I are going to try to talk to her tonight again."

"If she won't listen, what then?"

"Then we come up with a plan B." He looked at me skeptically for a moment.

"What are you?" I didn't know him well enough to share the truth, so I lied.

"I'm a witch," I said, looking him in the eyes. He tilted his head to the side and looked me up and down with an intensity that was deeply uncomfortable.

As an awkward silence settled between us, and then in a blink he was standing right in front of me. If I pursed my lips, I would kiss him. I took a deep drag of air through my nose; his scent was almost intoxicating. It was turning me on, and I felt my body heating.

Holy fuck, snap out of it, Ryan! You're acting like a hussy! I mentally bitch-slapped myself out of my thoughts.

"Next time you want to lie to me, try to do a better job of keeping your breathing steady and your heart rate normal. You're not very good at deception, are you?" He was looking me straight in the eyes, and I was rooted to the spot. I had to keep reminding myself to breathe. I couldn't speak, so I just nodded. He smiled; he knew what he was doing to me, and he loved it. Simon is attractive, don't get me wrong, but something just felt off, like it wasn't him I was feeling these feelings for. I couldn't explain it. "I must return to my people now, but I will be back soon. If you find yourself in trouble or in need of my assistance, just say these words."

He handed me a card with what appeared to be gibberish, smiled, and then he was gone. I put the card in the pocket of my sweats for safe keeping and prayed I never needed it.

After Simon left, I lay on my bed, thinking of everything that had happened. A week ago my life was normal—or as normal as it could be. I was so bothered that things had changed so much.

After arriving in Alaska, everything went to shit pretty much straight away. I started learning about my family's secrets, only to wish they had stayed hidden from me. My sister had changed so much; she wasn't even the same person anymore, and after the other night, I found it hard to imagine how we could ever have a loving relationship again. We had only seen each other a few times over the years, but we always talked and texted as much as we could. I thought that not having Mom around would mean we could finally have a normal relationship —how wrong I was.

I needed to figure what the hell was wrong with my sister. I couldn't survive the loss of another family member; she kept me sane through so much of my life with our mom. She would talk to me on the phone for hours when Mom was drinking or gone on a bender for a few days. Stevie would tell me, "Everything's going to be okay, you will be eighteen before you know it, and you can leave and come and stay with me." And that was the first thing I did when I turned eighteen and Mom vanished.

A knock sounded at my door and pulled me from my thoughts. "What?"

Alex poked his head in the door. "Dinner's ready, and Stevie just walked through the door. We have to try to convince her, Ry. I don't want to go against her, but if it has to be that way, so be it." His voice was just a whisper so the others couldn't hear our conversation.

I gave him a nod and stepped out of my room, trailing him down the hallway to the kitchen. As I entered, I saw Chase plating up the food, which smelled divine. I didn't notice how hungry I was until my stomach growled.

"Easy, tiger, dinner's nearly ready," Chase said, giving me a wink. I took a seat on the opposite side of the table to my sister.

Once I was seated, I looked at her and gave her a shy smile, which she returned. That helped relieve the tension in the air a bit. Alex took a seat beside Stevie, while Chase served each of us our plates. He had made an amazing spread: steak, potatoes, and a crisp green salad. I couldn't wait to dig in.

We all ate in relative silence. Every now and again, the boys would try to bring up stories from the past, trying to engage my sister and me into the conversation, but it never worked. After we all finished our meals, I pushed my plate away and exhaled a breath. I cleared my throat and looked my sister in the eyes as I began to speak.

"Stevie, I need to tell you something, and you must listen to me, because what I have to say is life or death."

"Like what, Ryan? Please do tell me what is so important." I gritted my teeth, not wanting to take the bait and engage in a fight with my sister.

"What you are doing with Randall Cane is wrong, and deep

down you know it. The fae didn't kill Jackson's father or our father, it was—" She cut me off before I could finish.

"You think you have the right to tell me what I am doing is wrong? What would you know about this world we live in? You are new to this life and know nothing of what lurks in the shadows. I am the leader of this coven, and I say what we do and don't do, am I clear?"

"If this coven is so great and powerful, how come I have never seen or met any of them then?" Stevie glared at me before answering.

"Because I have not allowed it. I will not take in someone who cannot respect the orders of their queen or someone who will embarrass our family. When you get over your insubordination and the victim act you play so well, then you will be welcomed into the coven, and not until then."

I was so shocked by her words that I couldn't answer her straight away; I kept opening my mouth and then shutting it.

"You have no right to speak to her like that, Stevie, and you know it. What you just said was a low blow and uncalled for. What the fuck has gotten into you in these past couple days? This is not you." I looked up to see Chase on his feet, chastising Stevie for her behavior.

"I am finally seeing clearly, cousin. Maybe you need to open your eyes and see what is going on around you. We are on the brink of war with the fae, and all you and Alex are concerned with is coddling my sister. If she chooses not to side with her people, then she does not belong here." Fuck that hurt, to hear my own sister say that I didn't belong. I was trying so hard to fight the tears that were threatening to fall.

"What are you saying?" Alex asked Stevie.

"She's saying that if I don't agree with her sealing the fae realm off, and start obeying her every command as my queen"—I said that last word with air quotes—"that I have to get my shit and leave, and I will not be welcome here anymore." I couldn't hold back my tears now.

"Stevie! You cannot do that; she is your sister, and you two just got each other back after all these years. You need to listen to her and hear what she has to say." Chase was trying to appeal to my sister, but it was clear her mind was made up.

"I have heard enough. Either she is on our side or she is against us. They killed my father, Chase!" Stevie screamed, and I could hear the heartbreak in her voice. My own heart hurt for her, but she was so wrong. The fae didn't have anything to do with our father's death.

"No they didn't! Randall fucking Cane did, Stevie!" I yelled back at her.

We were both standing at this point, staring at each other; her eyes were filled with disbelief and anger. Her eyes seemed darker, they were a dark green now.

"You're lying! Randall has done nothing of the kind. Ever since Jackson's father was killed, he's been the only one to see the fae for the blood-hungry monsters, and now that I am queen of the coven, I will be joining our forces with the vampires to ensure the fae never return to this realm."

My anger was reaching breaking point, and I could feel my magic rising inside of me. I took a few calming breaths to try to tamp down the magic burning inside of me; I didn't want to hurt anyone again.

"If you seal the fae realm, you will not only kill the fae, but you will also kill me. Randall knows this. He wants me dead, because he's afraid I'm the only one that can kill him." My sister just scoffed and pinned me with a death glare.

"And why, dear sister, would it kill you? And why in God's name would Randall be scared of someone like you? You have no control over your powers and cannot wield them. You are untrained and weak as a baby."

"Fuck you, Stevie. He wants to kill me because I am part—"

I was cut off before I could finish. The front door swung open and in walked Randall Cane and his enforcers, at least eight of them.

"What the hell do you think you are doing, Cane?" Alex roared.

"Keeping peace among our people," Randall said with a smug look in his face.

"What the fuck does that mean?" Chase snapped.

"It means that you are either with me and my decision, or against me," Stevie answered.

"Against you for what Stevie?" I asked.

"You either respect my decision and help us close the fae realm, or you are against me. I have the right to detain my enemy until I can figure out a punishment for disobedience," she snapped back at me.

"How could I be against you if I am not even part of your coven?" I tartly replied.

"Don't play coy with me, Ryan. CHOOSE NOW!" she bellowed.

I couldn't believe what my sister was doing. She was out of her mind, and there was no way in hell I was going anywhere with Randall. I looked at my cousins, seeking an answer as to what the hell we were going to do. Chase gave me a nod and a small smile; he was with me whatever I decided. I looked to Alex for his decision. He looked torn as to what he should do, but then he took a deep breath and gave a stiff nod. Alex would stand against Stevie, if it meant doing the right thing.

"I cannot let you do this, Stevie. I may be new to all of this, but even I can see what you are doing is wrong. I am begging you to reconsider." I looked to my sister, pleading with her to change her mind, silently begging for her not to do this and tear us apart. I just got Stevie back and now it seemed I was about to lose her again.

"You do not understand what you are asking, Ryan. I must do this for our people. It is our law—blood must have blood. You need to learn the ways of our people and fast. You will go with Randall until I can think of what to do with you."

"She's your fucking sister, Stevie! You can't do this. It's wrong and you know it," Alex said, exasperated with how my sister is behaving.

"Just because she is my sister does not mean the rules don't apply to her. She dares to defy me and thinks she can go unpunished!" she yelled.

At the mention of punishment, I could feel the magic coursing through my veins, and no matter how many deep breaths I was taking, I couldn't tamp it down. My anger was too strong. It was fueling the magic, and I couldn't stop it. One of Randall's men made a move toward me after receiving a nod from my sister, and as soon as his hand touched me, I exploded.

Blue light shot out from my hand, and he went flying back, landing unconscious on the floor. Two more men started toward me, and without thinking, I stretched my arms out toward them and they went sailing back, as well. One hit the wall with a cracking of plaster, and the other went through the window, sending glass shooting across the room.

"Stop now, Ryan, before you do something you cannot come back from!" Stevie shouted, but I was too far gone.

"Fuck you, Stevie; I will not let another person try to lock me away!" I spat at her. I was distracted for that brief moment, and when I felt two hands clamp down on my arms with a vice like grip. I screamed with rage. Alex rounded the table and shot a purple light from his hand, and my captor went sailing, unfortunately with me still in his grasp. Luckily, when we landed, he broke my fall.

"Run now, Ry!" Chase yelled while fighting with two of the guards. I looked to Alex, who was fighting another with magic. I went to make a run for the front door when Randall came out of nowhere and hit me hard in the face. I landed on the ground with a thud, hitting my head. I was stunned by both the blow to my face and knock to my head. I put my hand up to touch my head, where the thumping was happening and the shock of pain made me flinch. I pulled my hand away to see blood on it.

"You smell so good my dear," Randall sneered, hunger giving his voice a disturbing edge.

"Don't you fucking touch her!" Chase yelled from across the room. He and Alex were trying to get to me, but the guards wouldn't let up; they were all still fighting. I tried to bring my magic back by getting angry, but I couldn't feel it—it was just gone. Randall was on top of me in a flash, and I was pinned on my back, held captive by his weight. He leaned in close to my ear, his lips brushing my lobe, and whispered.

"I will not end you quickly. I will drink from you until you are within an inch of your life, then I will feed you my blood to heal you. I have a vast arsenal of ways to inflict pain on you. I have been waiting for you for *four* decades, and I plan to make you pay for all the years I was searching for you." He pulled back slightly so I could see his face, then he lunged like a cobra.

I screamed as soon as his fangs pierced my skin. He had a death grip on my head. I couldn't move. I heard my cousins shouting out my name, but I couldn't answer them. My eyes rolled, searching for help, and landed on my sister, who stood by, watching Randall drink, a smile on her face. The look of satisfaction on her face broke my heart. She wouldn't have to wait long for my death; I could feel my head getting light and my eyes getting heavy. I could feel the pull of death, and I welcomed it. Just as I convinced myself to let go, there was a whoosh of air, and Randall was gone.

I couldn't get my eyes to focus, and I was drifting in and out of consciousness. I felt an arm at the back of my head and then one under my legs. Someone was carrying me. I was trying to fight to open my eyes, but they refused. The harder I fought, the faster the darkness came, and eventually I couldn't fight any longer and darkness won.

Chapter Nineteen

I could feel the heat of the sun on my face; it was so bright I could see it from behind my eyelids. I smiled to myself, thinking it was going to be a beautiful day, when I was suddenly hit with the reminder of what happened the night before.

I opened my eyes to see I was on a bed—but not my bed. I peeled the duvet off my body and flung my legs over the side. It was then that I noticed that I was not in my own clothes. I was in a silk nightgown; it was a low cut one to. Who the fuck changed me?

I hopped of the bed and walked over to the window. I had no idea where I was. I was surrounded by trees and open land. I turned away from the window to further inspect the room. In the middle of the room was a beautiful king-sized bed that I had just climbed out of, two flanking side tables, and a rug at the foot of the bed. The room had antlers on the walls, and a small open fireplace at the other end, with two single chairs positioned in front of it.

I was making my way over there when I heard the door open. I stopped dead in my tracks and looked to see who it was. I let out a large exhale of relief when I saw it was my two cousins. My smile dropped when I saw who walked in behind them: it was Melakai and Jackson. What the fuck were they doing here?

Chase rushed over to me and pulled me into an embrace, I had to tap on his back a few times before he got the hint that I couldn't breathe. He pulled away to look at me, as if to make sure I was really here. I was then yanked away by Alex, who pulled me in for another bone-crushing hug. He managed to let me go before I had to tap on his back. We all stood there staring at each other for a moment before Jackson finally broke the silence.

"I am very glad to see you are okay, Ryan." I gave him a small smile in return.

"What happened last night?"

"You nearly died," Alex stated with a look of anger on his face.

"I thought I was going to die to be honest, I couldn't get him off me" A shiver ran down my spine thinking about how close I had came to dying last night. Randall wanted me dead and my sister never lifted a finger to help. I could feel tears welling at the back of my eyes, I felt so betrayed. Chase put a hand on my shoulder and gave me a gentle squeeze.

"We thought we were going to lose you last night until Melakai came and knocked Randall off you, He helped us hold off the remaining guards and escape with you. If it wasn't for him, you would be dead and we would be Randall's prisoners right now." Alex said with a look that was begging me to understand what Melakai had done in order to save us. Obviously Kai had told them that I might not welcome his presence.

He went against his king and his people to save me and my cousins. I looked past Alex and Chase to meet Melakai's gaze.

"Thank you for saving me last night and for saving my

cousins. I am forever in your debt, Kai." I couldn't hold the tears at bay any longer. Kai saved us, even after I rejected him.

"I couldn't help you when you needed it most, mi amor, but like I told you, I will always protect you from now until my dying breath." I could tell he meant every word; he really would lay his life down for mine.

"Where is Stevie? What happened to her?" They all exchanged uneasy looks, but Alex was the one to answer.

"She got away. By the time we took the remaining guards down, she was gone." My sister is a coward. The next time I laid eyes on her, the gloves were coming off.

"Where are we?" I asked no one in particular.

"We are at my home," Jackson answered.

"Why are you helping us, Jackson?" I thought werewolves and witches didn't get along.

"Because what your sister is doing is wrong, and I cannot stand by and watch her hurt innocent people. My pack is divided at this time; some want me to agree with her and the king, the others do not wish death on innocent people." I could tell he was conflicted.

"I am sorry that this is all happening to all of you. I wish I had more to offer but I don't. All I can offer you is my help." Each of the guys gave a smile and a nod.

"The first thing we need to do is try find a fae, or a way to talk to one, so we can get some answers and warn them about what is going on," Chase said

"I think Ryan may be able to help with that." Jackson was looking at me with knowing smile; dammit, he knew all along I had been talking to a fae!

"What is he talking about, Ry?" Alex asked.

"She knows one of them. I could smell it on her the night we came to the cabin to sign the treaty." They all turned to me expectantly, waiting for my answer.

"Okay, so maybe I have talked to one a couple of times, that doesn't mean I *know* him," I sheepishly replied.

"HIM?" Jackson and Melakai boomed in unison. I rolled my eyes at their reaction.

"Is there something you want to tell us, Ryan?" Chase gave me an accusing look.

I let out a large exhale and told them everything that Simon had told me. Their faces morphed from stunned to angry as I spoke. I knew they would be upset, but I never expected them to be that mad just because I had spoken to a fae. Melakai and Jackson seemed to be sharing a look of understanding between each other, but I didn't have long to ponder that look before Alex spoke and disrupted my thoughts.

"So this Simon that you have been speaking to, is there any way you can contact him?" I went to feel my back pocket for the card he had given me and remembered I wasn't wearing my clothes anymore.

"Where are my clothes?"

"We can get you some clothes soon, but answer my question, Ryan!" Alex snapped.

"I need my fucking clothes, Alex—it's the only way to contact him." With a nod of his head he turned and left the room, coming back a moment later holding my sweats and top, both of which were spattered with blood. I grabbed them off him and retrieved the card from my back pocket.

"He said that if I ever need his assistance or help that I should say the words on the card." I told the four men in the room, and they all nodded and told me to go ahead.

"I think it's in Latin or something. I'll try my best. *Azarah metronia openinga portass!*" As I finished saying the strange words, a strong wind picked up in the room. Chase grabbed my arm and pulled me across the room to stand by Melakai and Jackson, and Alex followed us.

The wind started swirling into a circle, and it grew larger, almost to the width of a car, and it was growing taller than Kai. The wind was so strong it pushed all five of us into the corner of the room. Then as abruptly as it started, the wind died down. On the other side of the portal I could see a beautiful castle and a large expanse of open land so bright and vibrant that it took my breath away. Before I could get too lost in my thoughts, Melakai spoke.

"It's a portal to Farrarie. If we wish to speak to this friend of yours, I think we must enter his realm."

"Are you crazy? We have no idea if they know about what our kind is trying to do to them. They may want our heads on a spike," Chase retorted.

"If we don't go, they could all die! This may be our only chance," Jackson snapped.

"The portal is shrinking. We don't have much time. We must go," Kai said, taking a step toward the portal.

"I'm with you; I just need to let Tyler know he is in charge and that I will be away."

I huffed. "We don't have time for you to do an errand, Jackson, and we won't be gone long."

"I can speak into the minds of my pack, love."

"Come on, it's closing" Kai said, grabbing my hand and leading me toward the portal. The others followed close behind us.

As we passed through the portal and made it safely to the other side, we all looked back to see the portal closing and the room we just came from disappear before our eyes.

"I don't suppose he gave you a get-home-safely card, did he?" Chase asked, and we all chuckled at his attempt at a joke.

"I think we need to make our way to the castle," I told the guys.

"We cannot go there; that is where the king is." State the obvious much, Jax?

I had felt pulled toward the castle the moment I stepped through the portal. I just knew we had to go there.

"I can't explain it, but we have to go," I said, not waiting for them to start walking.

"Fine, but the first sign of danger, we high-tail it out of there and try find a way home," Jax retorted. He and Kai both seemed more agitated than the rest of us, but I didn't have the energy to figure out what their problems were.

"Agreed, and do not touch anything. Everything can pretty much kill you here, according to the books I have read," Alex said.

"Nerd alert, nerd alert!" Chase whisper-shouted, and we shared our first genuine laugh in a long time. And as a group, we began our trek.

After walking for an hour, we came to a small moat. We were trying to work out how to cross it in order to get into the castle when a drawbridge came down. Two guards came out from behind the bridge with swords drawn. I couldn't fucking believe it. I thought we had gone back in time; these guys were in armor, like in the medieval days.

Melakai put his arm in front of me and started taking slow

steps back the way we came. Just as we all turned to run back the way we came, a whole fucking army emerged from the trees we just walked through. We were trapped.

"We can't fight them all," Jackson snapped.

"Chase and I don't have enough magic to even wipe a quarter of them out, and Ryan doesn't even know how to use hers to help us," Alex snarled in reply.

"We protect Ryan or die trying," Melakai commanded. I was going to respond when someone cleared their throat behind us. I spun around and the boys turned to the side, not wanting to turn their backs on the army behind us. I could tell they were all pissed that none of them sensed the army hiding in the woods. The throat-clearer was a beautiful young woman. She must be my age or slightly younger. She had pale blue eyes and beautiful white-blonde hair that was so long it was past her ass. She had curves in all the right places, and her skin was a pristine white, but it didn't look sickly.

"The king wishes to speak to you all, if you would please follow me?" she said and turned to walk back in the castle. We exchanged a look between ourselves, trying to figure out what to do. "You could always stay out here and take your chances with the king's army, I suppose. No harm will come to you, I swear it. The king just wishes to speak to you, and then you may leave." With a nod of my head, I started to walk toward the drawbridge. The others followed behind. I could feel the tension in the air— they were pissed that they had zero options other than to follow this girl.

Jackson and Alex shot in front of me, while Chase and Melakai fell in step behind me. They were boxing me in to protect me, and my heart swelled at the gesture. No one had ever wanted to protect me in my whole life, and now these four men were going to fight or die trying to get me out of here.

We followed the girl down long, winding corridors that

were lined with big wooden doors on either side, none of which were open. The walls were made of stone, and no paintings hung on the walls. The only light we had were the fire sconces on the wall. Clearly they were not set up for electricity.

As we rounded the fifth corner we came to a stop at the end of the hall, where there were two huge wooden doors that were guarded by two hulking men. They wore the same armor as the two men from the drawbridge. I swallowed loudly and felt a hand squeeze my shoulder—it was Chase. I gave him a small smile; he knew I was scared, and he was trying to assure me that we were going to be okay. If a fight broke out, I would not stand on the side and watch them fight for me. I would fight for all of them.

"Open the doors. The king wishes to speak with the trespassers," the girl said to the guards.

The two men opened the doors, and we followed the girl into what appeared to be a throne room. It was huge, with a long black carpet that ran down the center of the room right up to the foot of the throne. The benches flanking the runner were filled with people. It was like the whole town had come by to see the circus. I looked up to see a huge chandelier suspended from the ceiling, lit with hundreds of candles. There were six guards on both sides of the room positioned against the walls. The girl led us up to the end of the aisle and told us to wait.

We all stood stock-still, looking around the room. The people who had gathered were gawking at us right back. I saw a small girl with brownish hair and green eyes watching me curiously. When we made eye contact, she smiled, and I gave her a small wave.

"Rise for the king!" cried a voice from the room.

I leaned forward a bit so I could take a peek between Alex and Jackson's shoulders. When I saw him, I couldn't fucking believe it. The lying bastard played me like a violin, and I fell for it, because of his good looks and the way his voice made my body burn with need. I am such a fucking idiot. I watched as he stood before his throne and commanded his people to sit. Once they were all seated, he turned his attention to our group. He had a sly smirk on his face that made me want to punch him square in the jaw.

"I scent witches, a vampire, a werewolf, and something else I can't quite place," he said, amusement thick in his tone. I snorted, knowing my cousins would hate that he referred to them as witches and not warlocks. "Ahhhhh, the halfling does not agree. Why don't you both step aside so I can see her?" he said.

"Over my dead body!" Alex snapped.

"You either move, *witch*, or I will move you, the choice is yours."

"You can try, king, and its *warlock*!" Alex said with disdain in his voice.

"Have it your way, boy. Guards, remove them, and if they resist, kill them," he bellowed.

We all looked side to side to see the guards coming our way, Melakai drew his sword that I hadn't even noticed was strapped to his hip. Alex and Chase's hands started to glow, and Jackson started growling and snapping his teeth at the approaching guards, and his hands turned into claws. I could feel my magic well up inside me and my hands were glowing. I spoke for the first time.

"You touch any of them, and I will kill you all, mark my words. Your king will not save you from my wrath. We did not come here to fight; we came here to help you." I just hoped that they believed me. I don't think I could even kill a fly intentionally.

"Stand down!" the king shouted, but I could hear undercurrent of amusement in his voice and it pissed me off. It felt like he was laughing at me. "Come forward, little one." I put my hand on Alex's shoulder to tell him to step aside, and he looked at me, his eyes communicating the fear he felt on my behalf. I gave him a small smile and nudged him to the side.

"Hello again, love," the king said once I had stepped out from the cover of the others. I looked up to see those to beautiful violet eyes staring at me with amusement and desire, just like the last time I saw him.

"Hello, your majesty—or should I say Nico?" I asked the king. I could hear a collective sharp intake of breath at my words echoing through the room.

Chapter Twenty

The people in the room must think I have a death wish for addressing their king so informally. I turned to look over my shoulder at the others, whose expressions ranged from angry to confused. I guess both my dream boys are real—just fucking great.

"Hello, my love. I was wondering when I would see you again. I never thought you would have to use the card I gave you, but I would be lying if I said I wasn't glad you did. I just wish you had come alone," he said with a wide smile. Wait—what did he mean *give me the card?*

"Well I wish I could say that I was glad to be here, but then I would hate to lie to the king himself, even if he thinks he can lie to others." I heard more gasps, but I ignored them. "If I came alone then they would have hunted me to the end of the earth until they found me, so I thought it better to bring them along. Saves us all the hassle, you know. And what card are you talking about?" I said.

"Oh, my love, there is so much for you to learn. We fae can glamour ourselves." I must have had a look of confusion on my face, because he explained further. "It means we can change our appearance." With that said he changed right before my eyes and became the man I knew as Simon, the fae that visited me in the cabin back in Alaska.

"Oh, for fuck's sake, you lied to me yet again? What a fucking champ," I snapped.

"You will address the king in a respectable manner or lose your tongue, mutt," one of the guards boomed, stepping forward. A wall of four men closed rank in front of me, tense looks on their faces.

"You come anywhere near her or lay a finger on her head, I will end your life slowly" Jackson growled.

"Is that a threat, dog?" the guard snapped. Jackson moved toward the guard but stopped dead in his tracks when the king spoke.

"You will close your mouth and not speak unless asked to, Cyrus. How dare you insult my guest," he snapped.

"Forgive me, sire," Cyrus said stiffly before resuming his position against the wall. The king stepped down off his podium and walked toward me, and Jackson growled. Melakai came to stand beside me.

"If I wished to harm her, Kai, I could have done so many times. I am of no danger to her," Nico murmured. They stood staring at each for a minute before Melakai finally stepped aside and let Nico near me. He stopped directly in front of me, and his scent was so overwhelming that I had to take a step back. I looked up to see him smirking; he knew what he was doing to me and he loved it. Judging from the growl Kai let out, he knew what Nico was doing to me as well.

"All of you will leave us now," the king shouted, never breaking eye contact with me.

"But sire..." said Cyrus, who clearly couldn't keep his trap shut.

"I SAID NOW!" Nico roared.

Everyone got up and quickly scurried out of the room. Nico never took his eyes off mine, even after we heard the big wooden doors close. Chase interrupted our staring match by clearing his throat.

"Do you mind telling us why the fuck you gave Ryan that card if when she uses it you intend to kill us?" Chase asked. Nico finally looked away from me to stare at my cousin.

"Because the card was only meant for her, not for all of you," he said without an ounce of remorse. I cut Chase off before he could even reply.

"Why did you lie to me, Nico?"

"I never lied to you, love. You just never asked me what my full name was. Also, the glamour was for my protection, as well as that of my people, in case you chose to side with your coven or tell your sister I had visited you," he said with a shrug.

"What a dick," I muttered under my breath. I heard Melakai cough to try to hide his laughter. Alex, Chase, and Jackson did nothing to try to hide their amusement. I was angry and embarrassed at the same time. I couldn't believe that both the men I have had sexual encounters with in my dreams had deceived me. I thought I had made them up in my own head, but they were both real and willingly entered my mind without me knowing the truth. Nico just scowled at me and let out a huff of air before he spoke.

"My name is Nicholas Stone, but I go by Nico. Simon is just a persona I created," he said, shaking his head, like he didn't like having to explain himself. I'm sure he wasn't used to it either. He was a king—royalty never had to explain themselves, I suppose. I gave him a stiff nod in response. I was still pissed at him.

"Why the grand display of power when we arrived, *your majesty*?" I asked. He rolled his eyes at me for calling him "your majesty" but he couldn't very well say anything about it, because he was. Suck it up, buttercup. I have a lot more sarcastic remarks coming your way.

"When my scouts tell me that there is an unauthorized portal opened in my land, and that two warlocks, an alpha, and vampire walk through, with a being that scents as a witch but also scents as a fae, I go on high alert. What can I say?" Nico says while smiling from ear to ear, fucking arrogant prick.

"So you did all of that for show? Gather your people here just to show them how powerful you are?" I sarcastically ask.

"Well, no, they were already here, as I was briefing them on the coming war. You just happened to arrive at the wrong time, my dear" he drawled.

"We have important matters to discuss with you," Melakai said to the king.

"Well, well, look who finally got off the leash from his daddy," Nico replied. Kai stepped toward the king until they were nose to nose.

"Watch yourself, Stone. You may be the king, but you are not invincible," Kai snapped. Jackson caught Kai's arm and reeled him back to our group.

"You two need to grow the fuck up and put your past shit behind you," Jackson said to them both. Alex, Chase, and I all exchanged a look of confusion. They were acting like they knew each other—what the fuck is up with that? But before the other two could reply to Jackson's statement, they were cut off.

"Are we missing something here?" Chase asked the three men, who seemed to have some very big secrets.

I moved to the side where Alex and Chase were standing, making my allegiance clear.

"I guess I'll tell them then, but first, let's go to my study. It's a long story, and I'm going to need a drink to tell it," he said, heading toward the back of the room behind the throne. Jackson and Melakai followed him, while Chase, Alex, and I walked slowly behind them. Once we reached the back of the room, Nico opened a door and ushered us in.

The room was huge—it had stone walls with lit sconces, a large lit fireplace on the side of the room, and four couches set up at the back with a plush red rug in the middle. A huge oak desk was positioned on the other side of the room, but it was clear of papers.

Nico made his way over to a small table near the couches and motioned for us to sit. He poured himself a drink and offered one to the rest of us. I declined, but the four other men accepted a drink. I sat in the middle of one couch with Alex and Chase on either side of me. Jackson sat on the couch to our left, Kai sat to the right of us, and the king sat directly in front of me on the remaining couch.

"This is a long story, and no one else knows this story besides the four of us," Nico started.

"Wait—four? What four?" I asked.

"Yes, there is someone else, but we will get to him soon. Let me tell you how we all came to know each other first. Many years ago, there were two young boys who loved to run away from their duties and escape to the Earth realm for some fun and to watch the other supernatural kinds. They wanted to get a look at what the others could do—how they could wield magic and how they could fight. Also so they could go to a pub and get drunk." Nico and Kai both laughed at that. "One night the two boys snuck out of the castle and went to the pub. The two boys were drinking beer when they heard a fight just outside of the pub. When they got outside, they saw two young teenage boys being attacked by at least twelve humans. The boys could tell by their scent that the two getting beaten were supes, so they helped the two boys and ran off the attackers. Once all that was done they all stood staring at each other, not sure what to say or do, until one of the boys that was getting beaten said—" Nico was cut off before he could finish.

"Hi, I'm Jackson, and I'm going to be alpha of the greatest wolf pack the supernatural world has ever known," Jackson said, shaking his head while laughing, Nico smirked at him and then continued.

"One of the other boys from the other realm said—" He was cut off again.

"Nice to meet you, Jackson. My name is Melakai, but my friends call me Kai, and I am the right-hand man to the prince of the fae." My jaw hung open at Melakai's admission. I looked to my left and right, and felt a little comfort that both Alex and Chase had similar looks of shock on their faces. The king continued.

"The other boy that came with Kai then said, 'Hi, my name is Nico, and I am the prince of the north and east castle in Farrarie.' All the boys then looked to the other one that was standing next to Jackson and he said—" The king was once again cut off, this time by a whoosh of wind, and then out of nowhere, a man appeared. I yelped and dove behind Alex and Chase, who stood and blocked me from the view of the strange man. I could see through the gap between their bodies that the man had a cloak on, with the hood up so you couldn't see his face.

"Hello, my name is Dominic. My friends call me Dom. I am a hybrid, the first of my kind. My mother is a fae, and my dad is the alpha of the New York wolf pack."

"How the fuck did you get in here?" Alex asked the man.

"Clearly you weren't listening to the story, young one; I am the fourth member of this group, I guess you could call it. I was just filling in my part of the story; the others got to say their part, so why shouldn't I get to do mine?" Dominic asked, tilting his head to the side. "Now if you both step aside, I would like to see the young woman that has been causing so much trouble with my brothers."

"Why don't you take the cloak off and stop scaring her, then she might be more forthcoming and her 'boys' might step aside for you." The sarcasm was thick in Jackson's tone, but Alex and Chase both shook their heads stubbornly. I stood up behind them and pushed through the middle of their bodies. Chase grabbed my arm as I made it to the front of them.

"Take your hand off her now before I remove it for you," Melakai snapped at Chase.

"You need to mind your own fucking business, Cane. We cannot trust any of you with all the lies you have told, and especially your new friend that has just arrived," Chase retorted, I cut them both off from any further arguing by speaking for myself.

"I have to agree with my cousin. We cannot trust any of you. I trusted you, Nico, and you played me for a fool. The same goes for you, Melakai. You both have lied to us, and now you expect us to stand here and listen to more of your bullshit? I don't think so. Nico, thank you for allowing us here, and for the story, but we want to go home now! Also, new guy, nice to meet you, and hope you have more luck with these jackasses," I said as I headed toward the door. I looked over my shoulder to make sure Alex and Chase were following, and just as I turned back around, a figure appeared in front of me. I screamed.

"I did not mean to scare you, little one. Please do not leave just yet. You have not heard the rest of the story" Dominic said.

I had to take a few calming breaths to try to slow my heart rate. I felt Alex and Chase bristle behind me; they did not like our exit being blocked. I didn't even know how we were going to get home, but we would have figured it out, I'm sure.

"Why should we listen to anything you all have to say? All they have done is lie to me since I met them. Why would that change now?" I asked Dominic. He smiled and leaned down to whisper in my ear.

"Because, my dear, they will tell you the whole truth. They could not do that before, but they can now because we know which side you are on." I could feel the power radiating off of him... it was like a drug.

"Please let us explain further, Ryan, and it will all become clear. If you are not satisfied with the truth we tell you, I'll transport you back to the Earth realm and leave you be, I swear." Nico was pleading with me, and I saw the truth in his eyes.

"This is the last chance I will give the three of you; if any of you lie to me again, we are done. Do I make myself clear?" All three of them nodded and took their seats. I gave Alex and Chase a smile as I passed them to take my seat on the couch we occupied before. They followed suit. Dominic sat beside Nico on the couch in front of us. Once he was seated, he pulled his hood back, and a gasp escaped my mouth before I could stop it.

He was beautiful. He had silver-colored hair that was short on the sides and long on the top, but that wasn't the part that got my heart fluttering. It was his eyes. He had eyes that could see into your soul; they were magical, and the color was a beautiful violet color like Nico's, but brighter. His skin was so tanned that it looked like he had been kissed from the sun. His hair color and skin color made his eyes stand out like beacons. He leaned forward and placed his forearms on his legs. The cloak he wore did nothing to hide the muscles underneath.

"Would you like to hear the rest of the story, or should we just go on a tour and I can show you my room?" Dominic said with a wink, Nico leaned over and slapped the back of his head.

"Excuse Dom, he tends to think with his other head ninety percent of the time," Nico said while scowling at Dom.

"What can I say—when I know what I want I go for it," Dominic said with a smirk at me; I shook my head and laughed.

"Well anyway, before I was rudely interrupted for the third time—after all three boys introduced themselves, they went back to the pub to have a few beers and chat. None of them knew much about the other races, only what they had learned in books. The boys continued meeting secretly for many months, and they quickly became the best of friends. They even swore a blood oath to each other, which lasted for many years—until everything changed. Did you each want to tell your sides, or should I tell the rest?" Nico asked, looking from Jax to Kai and then to Dom. Melakai spoke next.

"I stayed with Nico for many years. I know we may all look young, and we have let you think that, but in truth we are all far older than you may comprehend. Jackson is the youngest of us," Kai said looking at me to see my reaction.

"If you were here with Nico growing up, does that mean you are a fae?" I asked.

"I was a fae until I was turned into a vampire."

"Why were you turned into a vampire? How did you come to be with Randall?"

"When the fae queen started seeing Randall, she thought no one knew. Nico and I started following her to the Earth realm and learned of her affair with the vampire king. We knew she was going to flee Farrarie, so I was tasked to follow her and guard her by Nico—she was his intended bride, after all. Neither of them wanted the marriage, for they never loved each other; they were only to wed for the purpose of merging both the kingdoms together. I followed the queen to your realm and guarded her until I was ambushed by a group of vampires one night and nearly killed. I didn't know at the time that the queen had begged Randall to save me, as she and I had become close friends in the time we were in the Earth realm. Randall did as she asked, thinking I would not survive the change, but to his utter dismay, I did. The reason I can walk in the daylight is because I was turned with fae blood in my system, and after Randall learned this, he would feed from the queen and draw some of her blood to feed his most trusted guards."

"Oh my God, so that's why you hate the name Cane?" I asked, finally understanding why he hated me calling him that.

"Yes and no. I hate the name because he forced me into the blood oath that I could not refuse, thereby making me his heir to the throne should he ever fall. It ensured that I would never be able to rise against him if there should be a war between the vampires and the fae."

"What did he have over you, Kai, to make you go against your people? And why can't you rise against him in battle?" I asked.

"He used the queen's life as a bargaining chip. I failed her and my best friend," he said, anguish plain on his face. "It is written in the blood oath that I cannot rise against him. I am bound by blood to honor that or I will die. Me being here isn't going to break the oath, but if I try to harm the king in a fatal way, the oath will take its pound of flesh."

"Wow, I never expected that. I just thought you were his loyal solider," I said, feeling guilty for assuming the worst of him.

"It is not your fault, mi amor; I gave you no other reason why you should think differently of me."

"But if you all broke the blood oath to each other, how can you not break it with the king?" I asked. Dom was the one to answer my question.

"The blood oath was broken when Kai turned. Technically he is dead; he has no heartbeat, so upon his change the oath broke between us, and more things changed." All four of the guys had solemn looks on their faces.

"Please fill in the blanks for us. How did you all stop being brothers or whatever you want to call it?" Chase asked.

"There were many factors: the fact that Kai chose being next in line to the throne instead of his brothers, and the fact that the fae killed my father," Jackson stated flatly.

"I never killed your father, nor did my people. I swear it to you, Jackson, if you would have just given me the chance to explain when this all happened none of this would have come to pass," Nico said, with such conviction in his voice that you just knew he was telling the truth.

"I never chose the throne over any of you. I never wanted it. I just made Randall believe that I did so I could better protect the queen and Sophia," Melakai said, looking Jackson in the eyes.

"But you failed, didn't you, Kai! She died anyway, and you still get to be prince of the vampires! The only reason he keeps you around is for fear that the queen's blood supply will run out, and then he'll still have you, a willing fae blood donor," Jackson spat at Kai. I saw Kai flinch at Jax's words; they were harsh and hurtful, and Jax meant every one of them.

"I never helped him kill the queen! I tried to SAVE HER!" Melakai shouted. Jackson stood from his seat, and Kai did the same. They were staring into each other's eyes, a silent battle of wills to see who would break first.

"That's what you say, but where were you when my father was killed? None of you came to my aid...not one of you. So much for brothers," Jackson snarled. He was making his way to the door when Dom spoke.

"The fae didn't kill your father, Jackson—the vampire king did; Kai has been working with Nico and me to try to bring him down." Jackson stopped dead in his tracks and spun around.

"How the fuck do you know that, Dominic?" Jax snapped.

"Because I followed him and saw him do it, Jackson. I cannot do anything to harm him, therefore I could not tell you outright—not that you ever gave me the chance," Kai answered.

"Okay, guys, can we cool down for a minute? Because we are not getting anywhere with this story," Nico said while motioning for Kai and Jackson to take their seats again.

"I will finish the story if no one else interrupts," Dominic said, and we each gave him a nod and he continued.

"Not long after Kai was turned, we all felt the snap in the line, so to speak, when the blood oath broke. I was here in Farrarie with Nico. We knew neither of us broke it, so we traveled to the Earth realm to check on the others. We saw Jackson with his pack when we snuck onto his lands, so we knew it was Kai who had fallen. We traveled to the manor of the vampire king, and what we saw through Randall's window was almost impossible to believe. Kai was on his knees in front of Randall, and we saw him drink from a chalice full of blood and watched his eyes change color. We knew then that Kai was not dead, but had been changed into a vampire. We waited for Kai to meet with us like we normally did every month at the pub, but he never showed. We couldn't contact him or see him. We tried to plan a raid to steal Kai from Randall and bring him back here, so we could have our brother back. We never expected that the night we raided the manor that Kai and Randall wouldn't be there. That was the night Jackson's father was killed."

Chapter Twenty-One

"So you guys all knew who killed my dad?" Jackson roared.

"No, we did not. We suspected that the vampires were behind it, and when we tried to come to you and tell you this, you tried to kill us both!" Nico yelled.

"Because there was fae scent all over him! How the fuck do you explain that? But you, Melakai, you have betrayed me the most. You knew and never said a word," Jackson shouted at Kai.

"I tried to tell you and the others, but you would never listen. You all hated me ever since I was turned. You never let me explain what my reasons were for the change. You just assumed I turned my back on you all," Kai shouted, his face a mask of anger. All these guys were so quick to judge each other and turn their backs, when all they had to do was just open up their ears.

"We all tried to tell you, Jax, but you were not ready to hear what we had to say." Dom spoke with such sympathy; you could feel how heartbroken he was for not being able to help his friend in his time of need.

"So that explains why Kai and Jax fell apart from you all,

but what happened between you two?" I asked, motioning between Nico and Dom.

"Nothing. Dom and I remained close. We tried for many years to help our brothers, but they rejected us many times," Nico answered.

"So when I told you all who the fae was that I was talking to, you knew who he was? And the reason you didn't want me to go to the castle when we arrived is because you knew who lived here, right?" I asked, looking at Jax and Kai.

"Yes," they both said in unison. At least they had the decency to look ashamed of themselves.

"Well, that explains why they were super uptight about the whole thing," Alex said with a chuckle. Jax and Kai shot him a death glare.

"Shut up, Alex. Why did you both come here, then, if you knew we were bound to see Nico?" I asked.

"Because I would follow you through the fires of hell, mi amor. I wanted to protect you. I thought Nico would punish you to hurt me," he said with a sigh and looked at the floor. I knelt down in front of him and placed my hands on either side of his face and lifted it so he could look me in the eyes. I didn't miss the growl that came from Jackson, or the snickers coming from the other four males in the room, but I chose to ignore them and focus on the broken man in front of me.

"Thank you for wanting to protect me, even if it meant fighting your brothers. I now understand why you did what you did when I was younger. You stayed away, hoping that one day I would be free of her and be able to live a normal life. You just never banked on me seeing my sister, did you?"

"I am sorry, but yes, that was my wish. I wished that Randall would never find you, because he would use you and then kill you." I could tell Kai was ashamed of his involvement in all this, and I hated that he felt like this.

"What do you mean *use her?*" Alex asked, always so observant.

"Her blood is the key to allow all vampires to walk in the daylight."

"Why her blood?" Nico asked Kai.

"Because she has the power of fae and witch, which means her magic is stronger than even Dom's," Kai replied.

"Holy fuck—so that's why he killed the alpha. He wanted to take the blood of all the leaders, so when he did eventually find the child, he had the most powerful blood to feed himself," Dom said with a faraway look in his eyes, like he was watching the pieces all fit together in his mind.

"Wait, if that's true, then that's why Randall is pushing the treaty, so he can crown the two new leaders. It was never about sealing the portal to the fae realm; he used Jackson and Stevie's hate for the fae to push them into agreeing with the treaty, and then he was going to kill them," I said, finally putting all of my puzzle pieces together as well. If Randall took out all the leaders and drank their blood, that would make him one of the most powerful supes ever.

"Fuck, you could be right, Ryan. I am sorry that I doubted you, my brothers. I was too overwhelmed with my own grief and the loss of my father to see the truth; will you all ever be able to forgive me?" Jackson asked, looking to each of his brothers. They all nodded and shared tentative smiles.

"Melakai, I ask your forgiveness, as well, my brother, for I should have never tasked you with the job of keeping the queen safe," Nico said, looking Kai in the eyes, with his hand outstretched. Kai looked at his hand for a moment then stepped around me and put his hand in Nico's. I took a seat on the couch next to the spot Kai had just left.

"You are forgiven, my brother," Kai said while pulling Nico into a bro hug.

"So, this whole time, you three have been working together, trying to bring Randall down?" Jackson asked. They all nodded their heads.

"Why have you all waited this long to try take him down?" I asked, feeling like it was the obvious question.

"Because Randall has something that belongs to us, and I need it back before we can take him out. He is the only one that knows where it is." Nico had so much sadness in his voice that it made me want to take him in my arms and make the hurt go away. *Where the fuck did that come from? I need to get my head back in the game.*

"What is it?" Alex inquired.

"Something of great importance to me, and I need it back." What could be so important to a king that he had to have this *thing* back before he went to war?

"So why don't you just ask him or make a trade? I'm sure he would give whatever it is back to you for the right price," Alex reasoned.

"No, he won't. I have tried for many years. What he has ensures that I will not attack him, even if he starts this war against my people."

"Then you are a coward, if you let your people suffer," Chase snapped.

"No, he is not. What he is doing is the right thing. You do not understand the circumstances," Dom snapped at Chase.

"Then tell us so we understand. We came here to help your people, Nico. My cousins have gone against their coven, and I have gone against my sister, who I love more than anyone else in this world. I gave her up for the life of your people. We have given so much up for the sake of you and your people; the least you can do is be honest with us!" I shouted. I was shaking, my anger rising. I couldn't stop it. I could feel my magic bubbling up. If they didn't start being honest with us soon, I was going to lose my grip.

"You need to calm down, Ryan, you're starting to glow," Jackson warned, taking a step toward me. As soon as I raised my hand to motion for him to stop, a blast of blue light shot from my hand and sent Jackson flying back into the wall.

"Holy shit, Ryan, stop!" Alex shouted

"I didn't mean to! I swear, it was an accident!" I snapped at him. I pushed my way past Alex and Chase and ran to Jackson. Dom, Nico, and Kai were already bent down beside him. I bent down near his head and lifted it so it could rest in my lap. I couldn't stop the tears from falling. I was a monster who hurt people, and I hated myself for it.

Jackson's eyes fluttered open, and he groaned as he tried to sit up. Dom placed a hand on his chest and told him to lie still for a few moments more. I bent over him so he could see my face and spoke softly.

"Jackson, I am so sorry. I didn't mean to hurt you, I swear. I am so damn sorry."

"Shush, it's okay. It's not your fault, Ryan. I know you didn't mean to do it. Now if you could back up so I can stand, that would be great," Jax said, looking to his brothers, who nodded and moved back. Once on his feet, he leaned down to offer me a hand up. I accepted it and let him pull me to my feet and into a tight embrace.

"You can let her go now, Jax," Nico said, irritation clear in his voice. Jackson let me go and stepped back, but his hands were still on my shoulders. I looked into his eyes and saw raw desire; it set my heart racing, but not for the reasons Jackson was thinking. Don't get me wrong, he was hot—but I didn't feel for him what I felt for Kai, and if I'm being honest, I didn't feel for Jax the way I did about Nico, either. Fuck my life.

Someone cleared their throat, which derailed my train of thought, thank God.

"Now if you two love birds would break apart and stop picturing each other naked, that would be great." Dom didn't apparently have a filter. I looked out the corner of my eye to see Nico slap the back of his head yet again. I moved away from Jackson and sat on the couch Jackson was occupying before I sent him flying. Dom took the seat next to me and everyone else took the same seats from before.

"I think you need to tell us what Randall has over you, king, before we risk our lives to save your people," Alex said.

"My sister. Randall Cane has my sister." Well that was a fucking game changer, now wasn't it?

Chapter Twenty-Two

"It all makes sense now; Kai couldn't come back after the queen died. He stayed with Randall so he could try and protect your sister. You sent your best friend into the lion's den to try to infiltrate Randall's enforcers, which he did. What you didn't expect was how far said bestie would go to protect the queen and then your sister. You have not retaliated to Cane's threats for fear of him hurting your sister. Kai followed us here with an agenda of his own, didn't you, Kai—you needed the king to think you came to Farrarie for me and not to tell Nico what you had learned," I said breathlessly. I knew I was right; I could feel it in my bones.

Dom started clapping beside me, and I turned to see the biggest smile on his face.

"They seriously do not deserve you. I swear, you are smarter than what anyone gives you credit for." Dom had such awe in his voice as he spoke. Wait—did everyone think I wasn't smart?

"What he means is everything you just said is right, all of it, actually," Melakai responded.

"Why did he take your sister?" Alex asked.

"Because she is my half-sister. Her mother was a witch, and Cane thought she was the one, but she isn't. Ryan is the one with pure blood," Nico said, looking at me with a sad smile on his beautiful face.

"So what does this mean for Ryan?" Chase asked

"That she can never fall into the hands of the vampire king, or a war will break out that might very well be unwinnable. I have no idea what the blood from you will do to his strength." I had forgotten all about Randall drinking from me until Kai just mentioned it.

"We need to make a plan, and fast. I will teach Ryan how to master and control her powers. I believe I am the only one strong enough to do that, and she needs to be ready, if her blood is supercharging Randall. We need a weapon of our own to beat him," Dominic said while giving me a devilish smile. That guy seriously had a huge ego and no regard for serious situations.

"But first we must send you all back. Dom will accompany you, and I will get to you as soon as I can." Nico didn't seem worried that my blood could potentially make Randall stronger then all of us. He just wanted us to go home. What a dick!

"Why do we have to go back now?" I asked, looking to the four alpha males in the room for an answer.

"Because I need to go back and explain my actions for saving you, so I can stay on the inside of Cane's manor. I also need to locate Sophia, before this war breaks out. Jackson needs to get back to his pack and prepare them for war. Dom will stay with you and your cousins to help you train. Nico needs to remain here and to prepare his people for battle," Kai said with a somber tone.

"Hang on a second—you just said she was your half-sister? And Dom said he was the first hybrid?" Alex asked the group.

"I am the first, because I can access both sides of my bloodline; I can change into my wolf form as well as use magic. Sophia can only use her witch magic, not her fae, so she is just a low-level witch, essentially." Dominic's answer seemed harsh, but it was the truth.

"I see. So does that mean I will be able to access both sides of my magic?" I asked no one in particular.

"Yes, you will be able to use both sides, with training. You have already shown how strong you are, but you are only using your witch magic, not your fae magic. That is why I will accompany you and your cousins home, so I can train you to use both sides," Dom answered.

"Thank you, I will try not to let you down," I said with a sheepish smile on my face, I looked over to Nico, only to see him trying to avoid looking at me at all cost.

"You will not let me down, sweetheart. I have faith in you, and we know you can access both sides already because you don't glow purple. That's the dead giveaway," Dom's answer explained why I didn't have the same color as my sister and cousins.

"We all have faith in you, mi amor. You just need to have faith in yourself," Kai said with such gentleness that it made my heart swoon a bit.

"How can you all be so sure? You guys don't even know me that well, and you are putting so much trust in me to save a world I didn't even know existed until a few days ago." I started pacing . These guys are putting so much pressure on me and what if I let them down, I would never be able to forgive myself if I let a world fall because I wasn't up to the task.

"Because I have been told that you will save Farrarie, I know someone who can see things. The fae realm will make it, with your help love." Nico seemed so confident that I could do this.

"I was just a normal teenaged girl a few weeks ago, and now here I am about to fight the only family I have left in this world —well, aside from Alex and Chase. But still, Stevie is my twin." I couldn't help the rising pitch in my voice as I thought about my sister. I was holding it all together as best as I could, but it was getting too much for me to hold in. I needed to get my shit together before my magic exploded out of me and I hurt someone else.

"Ry you are the strongest person I know. You have been through so much, and yet here you are, still standing strong and still trying to help others, even when no one helped you," Chase said, looking ashamed.

"Chase is right. Ryan, you are strong, wise, and selfless. You can do this. I know you can, because the cousin I know doesn't quit, and she sure as fuck isn't a pussy who runs away when shit gets hard! I know you are scared, and we all are too. We are about to take on the most powerful clans in the world, and the only way we are going to be able to even have a chance at winning this thing is if you man up and get your ass training so you can master your powers and help us win this thing." I looked Alex in the eyes and could see he believed every word he said, bolstering my confidence. With a curt nod and smile on my face, I gave both my cousins a hug and thanked them for their kind and empowering words.

"I feel like as long as I have your faith and support, I can do this. I think," I told the group with a forced laugh. "All joking aside, though, let's get the heck out of here and get our butts home and start training. If I know my sister, which I do, she will already be getting her soldiers together to shut Farrarie off from Earth." I don't like the idea of fighting against my own coven, but I had no choice. They were loyal to Stevie, and they had no idea who I was, or that I even existed.

"Then we need to move fast. We need every minute we can get to train you, Ryan. It will be hard, and you will hate me each and every minute of it, but it will be worth it once we win the war." Dominic had a look on his face that I couldn't quite place, and it started to raise the hairs on the back of my neck. There was something these guys weren't telling me. A quick glance at both my cousins they looked like they were wondering the same thing. Before I could even ask the question burning in my mind, Chase voiced it for me.

"What aren't you telling us? And don't bullshit me either."

"It may not even come to pass," Nico protested.

"Whether or not it does or doesn't happen, we have a right to know whatever it is. After all, we are planning to go to war against our own coven for your people." I agreed with everything Chase had said; I want to know what these guys are hiding.

"Tell her, Dom," Nico ordered with a sigh.

"You may be king, brother, but you are not *my* king, so watch the way you speak to me! If your sister does not surrender, Ryan, we will have to take out the threat by any means necessary." Dom cast his eyes downward, clearly anticipating my unhappiness. My blood started to boil, and my hands started to glow blue. Alex and Chase jumped back, and before I knew what I was doing, I raised my hands at the four men in front of me and blasted the whole lot of them across the room. Nico crashed into the far wall, and Dom smacked into the door and then crashed to the ground with a groan. Jackson was blasted through the nearest window, and Melakai hit the book shelf and collapsed the shelves, sending books cascading down on his slumped body.

"Holy fuck, Ry! You just smashed the shit out of them without even trying," Chase said with his hand raised in the air, trying to give me a high five. I just glared at his hand and he quickly dropped it and stepped away. I turned back to face the four men I just blasted; they were all standing now and dusting themselves off. At least they all had supernatural healing, so if they were hurt it wouldn't last long. I did feel bad about what I had just done, though, and at the same time I also felt good about it. If they really thought I would let them harm my sister, they were badly mistaken. I would never let anyone harm my sister, no matter what she has done or will try to do.

"We are sorry for upsetting you, mi amor. That was not our intention. What the others were trying to say is that we understand that Stevie is your sister, but if the choice comes to stop your sister or save a whole world, would you be willing to make that sacrifice?" I knew what Kai was trying to do, and he was right, but it still made me angry that he would even ask me that question.

"How am I supposed to answer that, Kai? Save a whole world or kill my sister—those are my only choices?"

"Ryan, we know that she is your sister, and that she is all you have left, but we are here too, and we are your family. I know it's not the same, but if it comes to it, you have to make the right call. Stevie knows what she is doing by siding with Cane, and that is on her, not you! She has made her choice, and now it is time for you to make yours, cousin." Alex was right; I needed to pull my big girl pants up and make the choice, but I would never harm my sister if I could avoid it, and that right there might just be my weakness.

Chapter Twenty-Three

"Now you all must go through the portal so I can seal it. Dom will be the only way to contact me until I unseal all the portals. I cannot take the risk that your sister or Cane will send an army through to kill my people before we are even ready. They won't make it far if they do, but still I don't want them here."

The only portal that would be left open was the main portal to Earth that kept Farrarie alive.

"I will go first to make sure that it's safe." Kai gave me one last look before he stepped through the portal, followed by Dom, then Jackson.

"I'll go ahead of you both." With a nod from Chase, Alex stepped through. As I was about to walk through the portal, Nico grabbed my arm. I looked up and saw those beautiful violet eyes pleading with me. I felt anger rise inside of me at the lies he told. He knew he was real when he came to me in my dreams, and he knew I was real, and never did he or Kai tell me the truth. I felt like such a fool, I gave them both so much of me in those dreams, and they lied.

"I know this is hard for you, but please believe me when I

tell you I never meant to hurt you, love. I had always intended for us to meet, but not like this." I couldn't bring myself to feel bad that he was feeling like shit; in fact, I thought he deserved to suffer. He and Kai both deceived me; they're not the ones who are feeling foolish, only I am, because they knew the truth all along.

"Now is not the time for this, Nico. I already have so much on my mind and so much to wrap my head around...the last thing I need is for you to fuck with my head some more. I will train and help you win this war, but as far as everything else, it's finished. Don't ever come to me in my dreams again. Do I make myself clear, *your majesty*?" I could hear the anger in my voice as I told Nico how I really felt. The worst part is that most of it was lies. I missed having fun with Nico and Kai in my dreams, and how they made my body feel. But now it just felt like what we shared was tainted by their betrayal.

"Yes, Ryan, you made your point. Just please promise me one thing?"

"What?" I said with an eye roll.

"When this is all over, will you give me a chance to explain why I came to you and why I kept the truth from you?"

"I'm not making any promises I can't keep, Nico, so if there is nothing else, I really think we should be going before the others get worried."

"Very well, love, be safe and look after yourself, please," he said before leaning down and placing his lips on my forehead. The touch of his lips sent a shiver down my spine. I could feel the heat creeping up my neck and into my cheeks. The bastard had a satisfied smirk on his face when he pulled away and I itched to send him flying once more. I couldn't fight my body's reaction to his touch, even though I hated it.

Chase clasped my hand, and we walked through the portal.

I never looked back, but I could feel Nico's eyes burning a hole in the back of my head, and that put a smile on my face. Once Chase and I entered my bedroom at Jackson's house, it was exactly the same except for the three alpha males and Alex standing against the far wall. I felt like I was a piece of meat in a lion's den, the way three of them were looking at me. We were stuck in a staring match until Alex cleared his throat.

"Now if you three are finished eye-fucking my cousin, you filthy pigs, let's get to work on a plan, aye?" Alex had so much anger in his voice that I think I even flinched a little. Chase had a glare plastered on his face, as well. It was no secret my cousins didn't like the men standing in front of us, but in order for this to work, we all had to get along, or try to, at least.

"I know each of you have issues with each other, but that needs to stop for the time being. I am not going to put up with you all squabbling like a pack of school girls." I made sure to look each of them in the eye as I spoke so they knew I was serious. They each gave a nod, agreeing to what I asked.

"I think we should start with the history of each race first thing in the morning. Take the rest of the afternoon to chill." Dom was looking at me as he spoke, and I gave him a thumbs-up. Not so mature, but I couldn't formulate the words right now. I was nervous as fuck.

Kai walked over to me and gave me a quick hug, like he knew I was breaking down inside and just needed to be reassured that we were going to be okay. He gave me a small smile and I couldn't take my eyes off his mouth. I wondered what it would be like to kiss him in real life. I used to fantasize about Kai and Nico being real...what it would be like to finally have someone who would love me and protect me. And now here they were, and things were so complicated that none of my dreams could be reality. A throat-clearing shook me from my depressing thoughts.

"Well, now that we got that sorted…it's been a long-ass day, and I think we could all use a bath and something to eat." Trust Chase to be the one thinking of food, but he was right—I was hungry and wiped out. Kai stepped back and faced Jackson.

"I will stay here with Ryan tonight to make sure she is safe." *Uh, a bit presumptuous, don't you think, Kai?*

"Oh like fuck you are. I will stay with her, not you, *enforcer*," Jax snapped.

"Now, now, ladies. I will be the one to stay with her, since you two can't get along," Dom said while winking at me. *What is up with him and winking?*

"Piss off, you horny bastards! No one is staying with my cousin. Chase and I will be the ones to stay with her," Alex shouted, motioning them to the door. I was getting pissed now—they were all talking about me like I wasn't even in the freaking room. That was about to stop right now.

"All of you can kiss my ass! I don't need a babysitter in my room, and do not ever talk about me like I can't make my own choices. I am a grown-ass woman, and no one will ever take away my freedom to choose what I want again! Do I make myself crystal fucking clear?" I was seething, and I know I went over the top, but I couldn't hold back. Control was my trigger button.

"Oh, Ry, I'm sorry. I never meant to upset you, I promise." I could see Alex meant every word he said when he looked at me; he was never a good liar—his eyes always gave him away.

"The only reason we want to have someone in the room with you tonight is because we're worried about your safety. Your sister or Randall could ambush you, and it would just give us peace of mind if someone was here to watch out for you. Please consider it." I never thought about it like that, and deep down, I knew that Dom had reason to be concerned. "You can choose who you would like to stay with you, if that helps, and just so you know, I am an outstanding big spoon." Oh my God, he was relentless. I sent him a glare in return, and he just laughed.

There was no way I was choosing Dom; he would never sleep on the floor, and judging by the way he was eyeing the bed I had slept in, he was thinking the exact same thing. I couldn't choose Jax, 'cause that would just hurt Kai, and the way Jax looked at me, I knew he wanted in my bed. There was only one man here I had eyes for, and I couldn't choose him either, because we had a lot to work out. Which meant my "choice" wasn't much of a choice at all.

"Alex, would you and Chase be okay with staying with me tonight?" My cousins both had a satisfied look on their faces, like they knew I was always going to pick them.

"Of course we will, Ry, we wouldn't have let you stay with any of these predators." Chase seemed pleased with himself after saying his piece. He walked straight past me and collapsed on the bed with a huge exaggerated sigh, just to rub it in the other's faces. Jackson gave Chase a look of utter disgust and growled. Before I could even comment on it, Dom slapped the back of his head.

"Dude, you really need to chill out. We all have to work together, and trying to kill Ryan's cousins isn't going to help anyone, now is it?"

"Since when did you become so mature, Dominic? Do not forget where you are," Jackson spat back at him.

"Well! Before this gets out of hand, we should all get cleaned up and then grab something to eat and work out a plan for tomorrow." Alex to the rescue—he was always the level-headed one of the family.

"Very well. I will send Tyler to get the three of you in an hour. He will escort you to the dining hall." With that said, Jax, Kai, and Dom exited the room. I made my way over to the bed and plopped down next to Chase. I was so exhausted. I really just wanted to hide under the covers in this beautiful soft bed forever. Alex made his way over to where I was lying on the bed, pulling me to him and wrapping his big arm around my shoulders. I leaned my head against his chest and let the tears fall. Alex held me while I cried, and I could feel Chase shift on the bed behind me and then he was rubbing my back, trying to soothe me.

"I am so sorry that you have to go through this, Ry. I wish there was something Alex and I could do to make this better."

"Thanks, Chase, but we can't run from this or hide from it. I need to woman up and get my shit together. I just don't want to hurt my sister. I still love her more than anything." I was sobbing more now just thinking about having to make a choice between my sister's life and the survival of Farrarie.

"Shhhhh, it's all right, Ry. Chase and I will always be here for you, and we will help you get through this." I was so blessed to have two such amazing cousins. They went against all they have known to help me. I sat up straight and turned on the bed so I could face both my cousins.

"I just want to say thank you to both of you, for all you guys have done for me over the years, and for what you are doing for me now. I know this can't be easy for you guys, and I just want you both to know that if either of you should want to return to your coven, I would totally understand."

"That will not be happening, Ry. We stand with you." Chase gave me a small smile which didn't quite reach his eyes.

"Chase is there something you aren't telling me?" He looked to his brother, as if asking permission to answer my question, and now my interest was piqued. Alex gave a small nod for Chase to continue.

"My family—I mean myself, Alex, Mom, and Dad—have had doubts about Stevie for a while now, even before your dad passed away. Stevie started to change over the last six months, almost like she is a whole new person. She stopped hanging with us and wasn't home whenever we would go visit her and your dad. Your dad was starting to get worried about her too—they were fighting all the time over him needing to step down as coven king so he could pass the title onto her."

I was shocked to hear this; Stevie had told me Dad was her best friend. "I know this is gonna be hard to hear, and for you to even believe us, but what I am about to tell you is the truth. Will you let me finish explaining before you go off your rocker?"

"I will keep my trap shut until you are finished Chase." I gave him a small reassuring smile, and Alex leaned over and grasped my hand and gave it a quick squeeze.

"Three weeks before your dad died, Alex and I went with our parents to your dad's house so we could discuss coven business. When we got there, the front door was open, so we all just walked in. We could hear shouting from the kitchen. Your Dad and Stevie were screaming at each other. They were so wrapped up in their fight that I don't think they even heard us come in. Stevie was out of control. She said, 'Mark my words, Dad—if you do not step down and let me take over, you will regret it. Ryan isn't even half the witch I am, and if you give her the crown, I will take her out as well.'"

I gasped, I knew where this story was going, and I didn't want Chase to tell the rest of the story, but no words would come out of my mouth. "The next week, Mom and Dad met with your father in private, and he told them that he was going to get you back from your mom and bring you home, so he could train you and pass the crown onto you." I couldn't sit still a moment more. I stood up and started pacing the room, mulling over everything Chase had just said. One question came to mind. I stopped and turned to both my cousins, and Alex must have read my mind, because he answered before I could voice it.

"He wanted you to have the crown, Ryan, because he never trusted that Stevie would do right by our people. He knew she was power-hungry. She even told us that she wanted to be the most powerful witch and rule all the races. She tried to convince your father to go to war against Jackson and Randall so our coven could rule."

Chase chimed in then.

"Oh and let's not forget about the whole marriage thing."

"Wait, what marriage thing?" I asked.

"Well, Stevie wanted to rule over all, so she thought that if she could get your dad to pass the crown onto her after he took out Jackson and Randall, she could then approach the fae king and offer an alliance through marriage." I was boiling now, and I could feel my magic rising. How dare she think that she could go and marry *my* Nico!

"What the fuck do you mean, *my* Nico?" barked Chase. Oops. With a sigh, I began to explain how I knew Nico.

"You know how Melakai came to me in my dreams?" They both gave me a nod, so I continued. "Well Nico use to come to me in my dreams, as well; that's why I knew who he was when we went to Farrarie."

"Wait—so if Melakai and Nicholas Stone have come to you in dreams, does that mean Jackson and Dominic have too?" I could tell Chase was pissed, knowing that not one but two supernatural's have been visiting me in my sleep, but before he could get me more upset, I answered.

"No, just Kai and Nico. I swear I didn't even know who Jackson was until I met him in the woods the day of Randall Cane's party—and I met Dom the same time as you guys did." They both seemed less tense after that.

"So anyway, back to Stevie—are you saying that because my dad wouldn't take out the other races and agree to give my sister the crown, she killed my father?" My voice rose to a high pitch when I reached the last part of my question.

"We don't think she did it herself, but we do think that she organized for someone to take him out." Alex wouldn't look me in the eye while telling me this, and I could tell from the tone of his voice that he regretted not intervening over Stevie sooner. I went back to pacing, trying to sort all my thoughts out.

I didn't want to believe anything that my cousins were saying, but what would they gain out of lying to me? I knew my sister had a thirst for power; I could see it in her eyes when we arrived in Alaska. To have our father killed, though—that was extreme. I needed proof. If I did find out that Stevie had our father killed for her personal benefit, I would go after her with everything I had, trained or not.

Chase, Alex, and I took turns getting cleaned up after our conversation. The shower here was to die for; I felt like I had washed all the bad away. Jackson had someone drop by with clothes for us to change into, which I really appreciated.

Tyler turned up a short time later to lead us to the dining hall, which was just a short walk from the room we were staying in. I could hear loud noise and voices coming from the double doors just ahead of us.

"My people don't take kindly to your kind, so stay close and we shouldn't have a problem." He had a satisfied smirk on his face that I just itched to slap right off. I knew Tyler didn't like us because we weren't wolves, but how fucking dare he judge us? Before I could retort, he pushed the two double doors open, and we were hit with the smell of roasting meat and the sound in the room amplified, almost as if the doors were acting as a sound barrier.

No sooner had I entered then the room went completely silent—I mean, you could hear a goddamn pin drop. I never liked being center of attention—hated it, actually—and right now I felt like I was a prized filly on show. I ducked my head down to avoid their stares, but I could feel their eyes burning holes into me.

"Put your head up, Ryan. If you want these people to believe in you, then you need to show them that you are strong." Chase murmured, and I knew he was right. These people were about to go to war because of my sister, and I was here in their home, asking them to fight with me to save a world that wasn't theirs. There were long tables and bench seats spread out through the huge room. I could see men, women, and children, and a broad variety of ethnicities represented. Before I could see more, a man shouted.

"The Alpha's bitch is a half-blood! Why would we help some low-level witch that can't even use her own magic?" I could hear the hatred in his voice; he didn't want me here, and I couldn't blame him for that—he didn't have any loyalty to me. But who was he to call me a bitch?

"You say anything like that again to my cousin, you hairy piece of shit, and I'll pummel your fucking face in!" I loved Chase for sticking up for me, but we were outnumbered here, and I didn't think for a second we could actually win if a fight broke out. I mean, there must be at least sixty people in here.

"What are you gonna do about it, witch, huh?" The angry voice belonged to a huge mountain of a man...I mean, this guy must be nearly seven foot, and he was all muscle, with shaggy black hair that just touched the tip of his ears and eyes they looked so dark they were almost black. We were about to find out what color they really were—he was making his way toward us, pushing people aside, to get to me and my cousins. By the looks of things, no one in here cared if he killed us.

I looked to Tyler for help, but he was just standing by with a smirk on his face. I made a promise to myself that if we got out of this hall alive, I was going to punch that asshole in the face. Before the hulk could make it to Chase, I jumped in front of him and put my hand out to tell the hulk-man to stop. Unfortunately, between the fear and adrenaline, I must have sparked my magic, because the hulk went flying across the room and landed on top of a table, which collapsed instantly from the weight of him. It was like it took everyone in the room a second to catch onto what I had just done, then the room erupted: the screaming was deafening, and some of them started throwing things. I put my hands over my head so I didn't get hit in the face by a plate that some lady just threw at me.

Chase pulled me into his chest and spun around so that he could cover me, but just as quickly as the roar started, the room fell silent once more. I peeked out from Chase's arms to see Melakai standing in front of us, fangs out, and body coiled tight, ready to fight.

"The next one of you that comes after Ryan will have me to deal with. If any of you so much as even looks at her disrespectfully, I promise you, your shifter healing will not be able to heal you fast enough." Melakai's words sent a shiver down my spine; I could feel he meant every word he said. Now I understood why he was the head of the king's enforcers—he was freaking scary when he wanted to be. And fuck me sideways if the lethal tone of his voice wasn't making me so hot and wet for him.

"What makes you think we're scared of you, vampire

prince? You may have a reputation of being a killer, but even the great Melakai Cane can't take on forty adult male werewolves by himself," jeered a woman with long shaggy brown hair and dull brown eyes.

"Ahhhh, Jessica but he isn't alone, love. He has me and two warlocks, as well as the strongest being alive on his side." God bless Dom and his power to just appear anywhere; he was standing right beside Kai. I straightened and stood on Kai's other side with my head held high, looking her dead in the eyes, daring her to make a move against us. If she had the power to kill someone just by looking at them, I would be dead. Chase stepped up beside me and Alex stood beside his brother, the five of us against all of them. I didn't like our odds, but I knew we would all go down swinging.

"Don't make me laugh, half-breed! You think that bitch standing there is the most powerful thing in world? Give me five minutes with her! I bet my life I would kill her in the first thirty seconds." A few people started laughing with her, and I felt my magic rise with my anger.

"You make one more threat like that, Jessica, and not even your father will be able to save you from my wrath!" It was Jackson who spoke, striding through the double doors. By the look on his face, he was pissed off at what had just transpired. "How dare you disrespect my guest like this?" He was screaming at her, and everyone in the room was bowing their heads.

Kai whispered in my ear, "All wolves must follow their alpha's orders. They are bowing their heads to show Jackson that they are submitting to him and don't want to fight. If you look an alpha or any wolf in the eye for too long, it is seen as a challenge."

"I have looked Jax in the eye a lot, and he has never tried to attack me or challenge me," I whispered back, but Kai didn't get a chance to respond as the plain girl spoke up.

"They aren't even pack, and you invite them into our home! You even let an enforcer in, the leader of the vampire king's army, not to mention two warlocks, a mutt, and a halfling," she said with a lip curled in distaste. I hated this girl already. She had no idea who I was or what the fuck I had been through in my life. I was done holding my tongue—this bitch was going down.

"How about I show you what this halfling can do with no magic?" I took a step forward to go over and slap that smirk off her plain face when Kai reached out and grabbed my arm. Jax let out a growl—who was he growling at, I wasn't sure. At that moment plain girl started laughing, and it had an edge to it that I couldn't understand.

"Oh my God, this is too good! The Alpha has finally found his mate, and she doesn't even shift. Does she even know that she is your mate, alpha, or have you not told her, in case she fancies the enforcer more then you?" I jerked my eyes to Jax and he tried to quickly mask his expression, but it was too late—I had already seen it.

"Do you wish to challenge my leadership, Jessica?" Jax was looking her directly in the eye, his tone icy cold. Plain girl went pale; she knew what Jax was doing. He was issuing her with a challenge, and by the looks of things, it was one she wouldn't win. She lowered her head and submitted to Jax.

"That's what I thought. If you ever disrespect me like that again, I will exile you from this pack." I heard gasps and murmurs around the room, but I couldn't take my eyes off Jackson. "I don't give two shits if your father is an elder and is on the council—he will not be able to save you from exile or my wrath. Do I make myself clear?"

Plain girl didn't move or speak for a moment; her head was

still down, and then she finally nodded and pushed past a few people blocking her way so she could leave the room. When she got to the double doors that we came through, she turned back and shot me a vicious glare. I gave her my biggest smile and waved. She screamed and slammed both doors open and made her exit. I know it was childish to taunt her, but I couldn't help it. After all, she did start it.

Chapter Twenty-Four

Jax lead us all to a table in the far corner. I sat down between Alex and Chase, and Dom, Kai, and Jax were on the other side. Dom was sitting directly in front of me and wore a sly smile on his face. I couldn't help but grin back at him—his carefree, mischievous attitude was infectious.

Tyler returned carrying some plates and was trailed by a small, frail-looking girl who must've been about my age. She had long blonde hair that was past her waist and the most striking blue eyes that were so pale they almost seemed white. She was absolutely beautiful, and I totally had a girl crush going on. Tyler set three plates out in front of the three guys opposite me, and then the girl set mine and my cousins' plates in front of us. That's when I noticed that my cousins couldn't take their eyes off her, either. Just as she was about to turn to leave, I felt an internal push to talk to her, one that I couldn't ignore.

"Hi, I'm Ryan, and these are my cousins, Chase and Alex." I pointed out who was who, and she gave each of them a shy smile and then finally looked at me. The moment her eyes landed on my face, her pupils went completely freaking white. Alex and

Chase jumped out of their seats and reached for her, but Tyler threw an arm in front to stop them.

"You cannot touch her when she is having a vision, it could harm her." I had no idea what the hell Tyler was saying, and the look we were giving him must have prompted him to explain further. "Aurora is a seer. She can see into the future and the past—it is a rare gift to have, and it is unheard of to be able to do both, so she is one of a kind." Just as Tyler finished explaining what was happening, Aurora spoke from behind him.

"You can move now, Ty, I'm fine, I promise." He reluctantly moved aside so we could see her, and sure enough, her eyes were back to being a beautiful blue. "I am very sorry I gave you all a fright. Sometimes my visions come on so suddenly." Alex stepped up and held his hand out for her to shake.

"Hi, I'm Al—" Aurora cut him off with a smile.

"I know exactly who you are, Alex, and I also know who you are, Chase," she said. "I have seen you both many times in my visions; you both play a huge role in Ryan's rise." Alex and Chase both looked at each other and then looked back to the blonde beauty standing in front of them. I pushed my way between the two of them so I could see her clearly.

"Hello Ryan, I'm Aurora." I stuck my hand out to her, and when she placed her hand in mine, I went icy cold, head to toe. I couldn't see anything for a moment, and then it was like a movie was playing: I could see my life from when Stevie and I were born, and then when my dad left with Stevie. I could see my childhood with my mother, and all the horrible things she used to do to me. I wanted it to stop, and I was screaming and begging, but the memories kept playing.

I could hear yelling in the background, though I couldn't make out the words, and I knew I couldn't take much more of this. The look of disgust in my mother's eyes was splintering my heart. I never wanted to see that look again. Just when I thought I couldn't go on, it cut off, and I could see the room again. I tore my hand from Aurora's and pushed past her, running toward the exit, tears streaming down my face. I was sobbing so hard I could barely breathe. I heard the guys yelling out to me to stop, but everything in me said to run, and I did.

Once I was out the double doors, I turned left and ran down the hall. Everything was a blur, and I was turning left, then right, then left again, until I finally found a door that looked like it led outside. I swung it open and spilled out into the yard. I ran right into the woods that flanked the yard. I don't know how long I ran through the woods, but I finally slowed when a creek came into view. My arms and face were stinging from scratches from branches that had slapped me as I'd ran.

I sat down on the grassy bank, buried my face in my hands, and cried. I was crying for the shit mother I'd had, and my crappy childhood; for my dad dying before I ever got a chance to get to know him. For the sister I just got back and then lost again. It seemed like there was always someone who wanted to hurt me, from my mom, to my sister, then Randall, and now the wolves. I just couldn't understand how I could be so disposable to everyone.

I was sobbing so loud I didn't realize people had arrived until one of them put a hand on my shoulder. I didn't know who it was, and I didn't care. Let them kill me and allow me to be done with all this. I just kept my head buried in my hands and continued sobbing.

Strong arms came around me and lifted me up. I moved my hands away from my face and saw that it was Jackson that had come for me. He didn't say anything, he just sat down and held me in his lap while I cried. His big, warm body was comforting, and before long my tears dried, and I was left feeling embarrassed that Jackson and the others had seen me break down. I couldn't see them, but I knew Kai and Dom were sitting on either side of Jackson. I could just sense their presence.

"I'm sorry for running out, I...I...I just couldn't... I mean, I needed air and I—" I couldn't form a coherent sentence. I was still hiccupping from crying, and Jax saved me from further embarrassment.

"You don't have to explain, sweetheart, I don't know what happened back there, but it must have been bad, because you ran out one door and Aurora ran out the other." I knew Jax was worried for both me and Aurora; I could hear it in his voice.

"Did you want to try telling us what happened back there, love?" For once Dom wasn't being a smart ass. He actually sounded really worried, which made me pause and look toward him. I could see the worry lines etched on his face. I glanced to my other side to see Kai giving me the same look. These three badass guys were brought to their knees by a woman crying. If this wasn't such a serious moment, I think I would have laughed. It was then I realized how I was sitting—I was right between Jackson's legs, with my back against his chest. I went to move so I could sit somewhere else, but Jackson wrapped both his arms around my waist and pulled me flush against him again. At this point I must have been as red as a tomato.

"I don't think so, little miss. You will remain right where you are until I am certain you won't take off on us again." I heard the smile in Jax's voice, and it made me relax a little. I let out a long slow breath and begun to tell them what happened between Aurora and I.

"When she touched my hand, everything went dark and then all of a sudden my entire life was all I could see, and it was like a movie. I mean, I could see from the time I was born all the way up to now. The memories I saw are things that I have been trying to forget for years. It was just too much to handle." I didn't want them to know what happened to me at the hands of my mother. Kai already knew some, at least, but I didn't want to share that with the others.

"What happened in your past does not define you. It may have shaped you into the person you are today, but that does not mean that you are your past. What you went through made you stronger and smarter in ways that no books would ever be able to teach you. You are like a phoenix, so you need to rise above the ashes of your past and sort through those horrible memories, because they are not you, Ryan; you are a badass halfling and heir to the most powerful witch coven in the world." I couldn't help but snap my head in Dom's direction—it was the first time I have ever heard him speak seriously. I felt Jackson turn his head that way as well, and from the rustling behind me, I suspected Kai was staring too.

"Oh, for the love of God, don't look at me like that. I can be deep and meaningful at times, just like the rest of you." Dom seemed sheepish after we all focused our attention on him, but his words meant so much to me. He was right. I wasn't who my mother said I was. I wasn't worthless, I wasn't a nobody. Mom wasn't around to hurt me now, but I kept letting the memories of what she had done to me define who I was. I knew I was changing and trying to make myself stronger by not letting others make decisions for me, but I was still a long way from being the strong independent woman I wanted to be. I still had nightmares every few nights, and I would wake crying and searching every corner of my room to make sure my mother wasn't there. I snapped out of my thoughts when I felt Jax rub his hand up and down my arm. I looked to Dom again and reached out to grab his hand; he let me hold it and gave me a faint smile. It was the first time I saw behind the cocky, arrogant façade Dominic projected.

"What you said—I...I... I want to be that phoenix; I want to rise above my past. But I think it will take me a while to fully get there." Dom gave my hand a reassuring squeeze and leaned forward to tuck a strand of hair behind my ear with his free hand. A part of me expected to hear Jax start growling, but he remained silent. Dom's hand lingered longer then it needed to, and part of me didn't want him to move his hand away, but the other part of me knew it was wrong having him touch me like that while sitting in another man's lap. Dom finally let his hand drop with a reluctant sigh, and I pushed myself off Jackson's lap. I started pacing up and down the river bank, with the guys sitting there watching me, looking slightly amused at my repetitive path.

I had no idea what I was going to do, but I knew I had to at least try and learn how to use my powers in order to help Nico. I wasn't going to run anymore; I was going to stand and fight for once in my life. I was tired of always being scared. It was time for me to be the person my father clearly thought I was and fight for what I know is right.

"Okay. I'll do whatever I need to so I can be ready to help Nico," I said to all the guys.

"Oh, so you're just helping Nico, doll?"

"What are you on about, Dom?" I asked, confused by his question. I was trying to help save a whole world not just one person.

"Well, love, you said just NICO, not Farrarie, so I was just thinking maybe you only wanted to help for Nico's sake." Dom was laughing now, I mean full on belly-laughing, and here I am trying to hide my shame. I knew I was blushing; there was nothing I could do about it though, so I just glared at Dom.

"Shut up, you idiot!" Jax slapped the back of Dom's head "You need to learn how to filter shit before you say it, dumbass." He turned back to me. "We know you want to help the whole of Farrarie and not just Nico, love. Ignore Dom, he's an idiot."

I appreciated Jax so much in this moment for turning the

attention away from me that I walked right up to Jax and gave him a hug. I felt him tense for a second then relax, and he circled his arms around my waist and buried his head in the crook of my neck.

I could hear Dom mumbling about Jax being a suck-up, but that's not what stopped our hug—it was Kai. Kai pulled Jax away from by the back of his shirt with enough force to throw him on the ground. I was shocked by his display of anger. I could feel the jealousy rolling off him in waves.

"Unless you want me to put his fucking head through a tree, I would restrain from touching him again."

Jax was on his feet and furious. "You ever fucking touch me like that again, you blood-sucking leech, and I will tear your fucking heart out. Well, what's left of it, anyway," Jax sneered. Kai spun around and stepped toward Jax, and I couldn't suppress my short scream of frustration.

"I am no one's, Melakai—do you understand me?" Both Kai and Jax shifted their attention back to me. "I am standing right here! You have no right to tell anyone they can or cannot touch me. That is *my* choice." I was shaking now, and I could feel my anger rising higher and higher the longer I looked at Kai.

"Ry, sweetie, you need to calm down. You're starting to glow." Dom was right, I realized. I could see my hands were glowing. "Deep breaths, babe, in and out. Just focus on me, okay? Just look at me, Ry." I did as Dom said and kept my eyes on him, breathing in and out for a few moments to regain my composure. "Good girl. Do you feel better now?" I gave Dom a curt nod.

"I think we need to head back now." Jax had a look of pure torture on his face—something was wrong.

"What's wrong?" I asked Jax.

"Nothing, we just need to head back, is all." *Liar,* I think to myself. The walk back to the compound was silent, all of us lost in our thoughts.

Chapter Twenty-Five

Once we got back to the compound, Jax lead us on a winding path through the biggest building and stopped at a set of massive oak doors. Jax ushers us all into the room, and I nearly gasped when I got inside. The room was huge, and lined with bookshelves floor to ceiling, complete with a sliding library ladder. There was a huge wooden desk in front of beautiful bay windows that overlooked a section of the forest, and a lovely sitting area with enough seating for all of us and then some.

"Please have a seat. I will get one of my pack members to bring in some drinks and food." Bless you, Jackson Marshall, you read my mind; I was so hungry my stomach actually ached. Jackson led the way over to the couches and took a seat at the far end, closest to the fireplace. Dom sat on the same couch as Jax. I sat on one of the couches that Kai was occupying, but I made sure to sit all the way on the other end.

"Right, well, let's get down to it, shall we?" Jackson always sounded so businesslike; he needed to let loose a little.

"Well, we can't attack Randall without rescuing Nico's sister first." I couldn't help thinking of what this poor girl has gone through at the hands of Randall Cane. "Second, we have to stop Stevie. We cannot let her help Randall destroy a whole world. We must try to reason with her first, before other drastic measures are taken." I knew Jax was right, but hearing him talk about "other ways" to stop my sister was very unsettling.

"Are you okay, mi amor?" I could hear the concern in Kai's voice.

"Yes, I'm fine, thank you." I couldn't look him in the eye; he would know straight away that I wasn't okay, and I didn't want anyone's pity, nor did I need it. I took a deep breath and shoved everything I was feeling deep down inside of me. I would deal with all of that later; there was no time for me to even try sort through everything I was feeling. Before we could continue with our discussion, the door opened and my cousins walked in. They both sat on the couch opposite Kai and me, and we filled them on what we had just discussed.

"I think the first thing we need to do is start training Ryan and get her familiar with her powers. Then we need to get everyone else training and preparing for the war that is to come. We won't be able to call on other clans, as the witches answer to Stevie. We can't call on any vamps, either, as Randall will find out." Everything Jackson had said only highlighted the struggle ahead for us.

"I can call on all the packs, as they answer to me. I will call the elders here for an emergency meeting to ask them for their help; it will be no easy task to sway them, so we need to make sure Ryan is able to showcase her powers for them, to be able to believe that she is indeed the chosen one." Wow, no fucking pressure then. "We will also need to make lodging arrangements for the packs willing to fight for our cause. I am not like Randall; I will never force my people to fight a battle they do not wish to fight. I ask that you all show some respect to those who wish not to take part in this war."

"How long do we have to get her ready?" Alex asked.

"You have about two weeks." The whole room erupted, everyone was shouting and yelling to the point I couldn't understand a word any of them were saying. I was about to walk out of the room when suddenly everyone stopped yelling and looked to the door. Aurora was just standing in the entryway; she looked so small and fragile, with her hands clasped in front of her and head slightly downcast, yet she was still so lovely. Jackson stood to make his way over to her, but then she spoke, and her words stunned us all.

"The time frame you have given is long enough; you will all be ready. But none of you will be training Ryan right away. She has another path to take before then, I have foreseen the struggles she will face. It will be hard on her, you will want to quit Ryan. Just know that the struggles that are coming will end, please remember that. My vision also tells me she must marry in order for her powers to truly be unstoppable—only by uniting two worlds will you be able to stop the war from ending all supernatural's." I swear to God that you could have heard a pin drop in the room.

I looked around the room, almost wanting to laugh at the stunned looks on the faces of the men, but when I looked back to Aurora, she had a look of such pity and it sparked my fury.

"I know this is hard to hear, bu—" I cut her off, not wanting to hear what she had to say. Hasn't she already said enough?

"You have no idea what the fuck I am feeling, and I don't know how to believe you after that trick you pulled on me today."

"You may not think so right now, but believe me I *do* know how you feel. Like you, my future has already been planned for me. I will marry someone I do not love either, Ryan, but for the greater good I will do what needs to be done. You can either fight me on my vision, and we all die, or you can try to understand that marrying to save lives rather than for love will be the only way we all live."

What the fuck was I supposed to say to that? "My brother is not thrilled with my future outcome either, and chooses not believe it will happen, but I have never been wrong. I am asking you to please trust me and let me guide you through this, as I am the only one in this room that can help you unlock the other half of your powers." Before she could continue, Dom interrupted.

"How in God's name do you know how to help her unlock the other half of her powers?" Everyone was waiting for her answer.

"Because I know who put the lock on her powers, and he also showed me in the vision from the past how to unlock said gift, if the time ever came."

"Wait—you said he?" Trust Kai to only hear the "HE" out of everything she said. I rolled my eyes at his nonsense.

"Yes, Mr. Cane." Aurora was looking at me like I should know who "he" was, but I had no idea who she was talking about. Then out of nowhere, the answer hit me.

"It was my dad, wasn't it?"

"Yes, Ryan, it was the last gift he gave you." I wanted to drop to my knees at the thought. "He also left you a message, I don't know how he knew that you would meet a seer, but what he has to say will hurt you, so you must be prepared." I didn't think I would ever be ready for anything my dad had to say to me; I still haven't opened the letter he left for me. I left that letter in my room at the cabin, I may never know what he had written now.

I sighed. "Okay, Aurora, let's do this." I wasn't sure why my dad would put a lock on my powers, but I knew he would have only done it to protect me.

"You all need to back up, please, so I can begin. Ryan, I need you to relax and take a few deep breaths and just try to open your mind. I know it's hard, but if you could just try it would make it a lot easier and less painful for you." I tried to ignore the feeling of being watched and concentrated on clearing my mind and letting Aurora in.

"Ryan, I'm going to touch your hand now, and I need you to try not to resist or it will hurt you. It won't be like before." I didn't understand what she meant. "I'm trying to show you a memory, not read your thoughts, so it's a bit trickier." Dear God, what the hell have I gotten myself into? Before I could ponder that thought at any length, I felt a stabbing pain in my head and a cry tore out of my mouth. I heard a commotion, but I couldn't move—I couldn't even open my eyes; it was like my body was frozen in place.

"Ryan, I know you're scared, but just breathe and try to relax. I'm going to try and push the memory into your mind again. Don't try to resist or it will hurt. Just breathe and try to let me in. If at any time you want me to stop, just say so." I took three big gulps of air and tried to relax as much as I could, focusing solely on letting my mind be blank and open.

I didn't feel a thing this time, I just saw it. Once again it was like a movie was playing in my mind, but this was one I hadn't seen before. All I had to do was focus and I could hear and see everything, and then that's when I saw him. I saw my dad.

Chapter Twenty-Six

I could see him! I could freaking see him, and I burst out crying. He was right there in front of me like I could touch him. His brown hair was the same as I remembered, long on the top and short on the sides, and his eyes had so much love in them. I remember those big beautiful green eyes; when he looked at me as a kid, I always knew I was loved. His eyes told the story that he couldn't. I don't remember this ever happening—I must have been like eight or nine. My mind went blank then, and I was transported back to the time this memory occurred.

I couldn't believe it! Daddy had come to see me. I hadn't seen him in so long, and I missed him so much. Daddy picked me up from school early and took me to get ice cream, and we went to the park. I never got to go to the park; Mommy always made me go straight to my room when I got home. I shivered thinking about what Mommy does when she's angry with me, but I didn't want Daddy to know that Mommy hurts me. It might make him mad at me too. I was sad that Daddy didn't bring Sissy to play, but he said he wanted to spend time with just me. Daddy pushed me on the swings and watched me play on the slide and helped me on the monkey bars. I was having so much fun, and I never *wanted this day to end. I was playing in the sand pit when Daddy called out to me. He was sitting on the picnic table that was under the really big tree.*

"Ryan, come here a minute, sweetheart. Daddy wants to talk to you." I quickly got out of the sand pit and ran over to Daddy, climbing onto the bench seat opposite him. "I need to talk to you, sweetheart, and I need you to listen to Daddy. I know it will be hard for you to understand, but when you're older, a seer will show you this."

"What's a seer, Daddy?"

"You will find out when you're older. For now I need you to just listen to Daddy, okay?" I nodded my head so he would continue. "You are a very special girl—one of a kind. You and Stevie may be twins, but you are so very different. One day when your older you will feel like there is something missing or that there is a part of you that needs to be set free, and when that times comes, that is when you will know that you are ready to unleash the other half of you that's waiting inside. I hope when that time comes, I will be here to help guide you, but just in case, I'm telling you now. Your sister isn't like you; she is not strong enough to hold both influences. I will continue to try to guide her, but I feel that she is already too hungry for power. I know this all sounds mixed up and confusing, but I promise it will all make sense one day." I didn't know what Daddy was saying—it was all so hard to understand—but I didn't want Daddy to think I was dumb, so I just nodded my head like I knew exactly what he was saying. "One day you will have to make a choice, Ry, and that will be the hardest choice of them all; what you can do is so extraordinary but also such a burden. Your blood is the key to seal a world. It is also the most potent power enhancer in existence. Anyone that drinks from you will become virtually invincible. If that day should come, only you will be able to stop it—well, with the help of a bloody fairy."

Daddy didn't sound like he liked fairies at all. I was shocked; I loved fairies.

"What I'm trying to say, Ryan, is you need to learn how to harness and control what you are. Your gifts are tuned to your emotions, so if you have a meltdown, it could really harm a lot of people unless you learn to control it. I have seen that in the future you will meet a group of men who can help you, but only one of them can help you unlock who you really are.

When that day comes, it will be so overwhelming and so hard to control, but you must try, okay?

No matter how hard or how painful it is, you must try to push through it. You need to control the power inside you, if you don't it will consume you. Stevie will not be there to guide you; I have seen it, and it hurts me to know that my two girls will be on opposite sides of the war to come. You need to save your sister, Ry. She will need you more than ever. Promise me that when that time comes to pass, you will do everything you can to save your sister. Promise me, Ryan, that you will save Stevie!" I was scared. I didn't know why Stevie would need saving, but I loved my sister, she was my other half, so of course I would do whatever it took to keep her safe.

"I promise, Daddy. I will always protect Stevie, no matter what." The look in my father's deep green eyes was so sad that it scared me. I didn't understand why he would look like that.

"If there is ever anything you need to know, go to a man named Nico. He is a friend of mine. When you get older you are destined to meet. He can answer the questions you will have. I will always hate myself for the way things ended up. I know what your mother is like, and believe me, I wish I could take you away from her." I could see the look of defeat on Daddy's face and I hated he felt that way. I knew then it was best that Daddy never know what Mommy had done to me. I leaned across the table and grabbed Daddy's hand. "I wish with all my heart that you could *remember this day and this talk so that you would know that I have always been here watching over you and loving you since the day you were born. I will always be here for you, and when the time comes, I will be here to help you understand what you are and where we come from. Your mother doesn't understand what we are and doesn't want to. I tried so hard and for so many years to help your mother, but nothing I did could get through to her. She has so many demons inside her mind that she is trying to fight."* I knew better than Daddy did about Mommy and her *"voices"*—she said they always told her that I was evil and needed to be put down.

"I love you Ryan, that's why I need you to remember that the key to unlock what you need is within you. You will need another to help balance the power; you need to merge two worlds to unlock your gifts. Just remember to focus and harness it, and most importantly embrace what you are, because you are strong and smart. You will know what to do. The answers you seek are within you. I love you, my baby girl. My princess.

Chapter Twenty-Seven

I came back to the present with tears rolling down my face. I never remembered that talk or that day—God, I wish I did remember. That would have been the last time I saw my father properly. I couldn't hold the sobs back; the tears just kept flowing. I knew as soon as I opened my eyes I would see so many pairs of eyes on me, and I wasn't ready to face all the questions. I felt strong arms engulf me, and I knew straight away that it was Kai, and as much as I hated to admit it, his embrace made me feel so grounded, like I could get through this and find whatever the key was inside myself. If my dad thought I could do this and unlock the power inside me, then I would, do it for him as well as for Farrarie.

"I've got you, mi amor." I couldn't speak past the lump in my throat, so all I could do was nod my head against Kai's chest. He didn't push me for an answer or ask what happened; he just held me, and it meant more to me than he would ever know.

"Aurora are you okay?" Oh my God, in my selfishness I completely forgot about her and the toll it must have taken on her showing me the memory. I pulled away from Kai and started to dry my eyes.

"I'm fine, just a bit tired, Jax."

Kai reluctantly pulled away from me with a sigh and stood up to move out of my way. I saw Aurora sitting on the chair directly in front of me. She looked exhausted. I was so absorbed in my own drama that I didn't even think about the toll it would take on her.

"Thank you, Aurora. You have no idea what a beautiful gift you just gave me." I felt more tears threatening to spill, but I forced them back. Now was not the time or the place for me to break down.

"It was my pleasure, Ryan. You are so much stronger than you know. You will be our savior, and if what I have seen comes to pass, you may change my future as well."

"What do you mean *I can change your future?*" She just responded with a sweet little smile. A smile is not a fucking answer, woman! Give me a little something to work with. I could see Alex and Chase sitting nearby with worried looks. I knew I would have to explain what I saw to everyone, but I just wasn't ready. Kai, Jax, Dom, and Tyler were in the corner having a private conversation that I just knew was about me.

"If you guys want to stand in the corner like school girls and talk shit about me, at least say it to my face," I said loudly. All four guys had the decency to look guilty.

"Forgive us, love, we were just trying to figure out what we should do from here." Trust Dom to come up with the million dollar questions of the year; I couldn't answer his question so I just shrugged.

"Ry, I understand that what you saw must have been hard, but if there is anything you need, or want to talk about, Chase and I are here for you." Bless Alex—I would be so lost without my cousins.

"Thank you both, but I think the only person who can answer my questions is Nico." I saw the look of shock cross everyone's faces—except for Aurora, obviously she knew why I needed Nico.

"Why the hell do you need that dick?" Chase grumbled.

"Because Dad said I needed Nico." I saw a flash of anger cross Kai's face, almost like he felt betrayed, but I couldn't bloody well help that Nico knew my dad, now can I?

"Well, I did not see that coming"

"I don't think any of us did Dom" Jax started pacing, and I had no idea why he was anxious. I should be the one up and pacing, not him. "If Nico knew your dad then that means he lied to us again."

"How can you be sure? Maybe he was sworn to keep a secret for an old friend." Trust Dom to be the voice of reason and on Nico's side.

"I knew he would never change," Kai growled.

"How do you know that, Melakai? Maybe he was trying to protect the girl's feelings." I never thought I would see the day that Tyler ever stuck up for the king. I knew he hated other supes. I don't think I was the only who thought that either by the looks on everyone's faces, they were all thinking the same thing. "Why are you all looking at me like that?"

"Oh my God, Ty, because no one ever thought you would care to defend any other supes ever!" Aurora responded with exasperation.

"Don't make a big deal out of it, okay? It won't happen again, trust me." I couldn't help but laugh at Tyler's red face, he was embarrassed. I had never seen the big wolf blush before. Everyone else joined in and was laughing, and Tyler was getting so pissed at all of us. "That is the last time I try and be nice to anyone other than my kind" with that said Tyler turned and stomped out of the room like a child. Not letting Tyler's departure deter our group from the main problem, Alex spoke.

"Okay, well, we need to get Nico here and have a chat with

him." the only one who could get a hold of him was Dom, so it was all resting on Dom to get Nico here so I could demand answers.

"Okay, I'll see what I can do. I'm going to need some time, as he has sealed all the portals. I can open one, but Nico will have to allow the portal to open in Farrarie."

"What do you mean allow you to open a portal?" Chase took the words right out of my mouth.

"Nico needs to allow my magic into Farrarie, because if I just force it then I could end up shattering the magic he has sealing the other portals. It's hard to explain but it will be easier if I just reach out to Nico with my magic and he just accepts it and lets me have access to Farrarie so I can bring him here. No one can know Nico is here—I mean no one." Dom was starting to make me worry, so I had to ask.

"Why can't anyone know Nico is here?"

"Because if by some chance there is a traitor in our midst, then they will know that Farrarie is unguarded by the king, or they could come here and try and fight to take Nico. Nico would give up his life to save his people, and I don't want my brother dying anytime soon, Ryan." I gave Dom a stiff nod; it wasn't very often that Dom was serious, so I knew he meant business.

Everyone left the room to give Dom time to prepare whatever he needed to in order to get Nico here, agreeing we would meet back in Jax's office in an hour.

With an hour to kill, I decided to ask Aurora if she would take a walk with me. I needed time alone with the seer to pick her brain about this whole marriage thing. The guys were reluctant to let us go wandering around by ourselves, so I said that we would go to my room and talk there. They were hesitant but eventually agreed. Once we were safely inside my room, the questions just came pouring out.

"You need to help me understand some things. Why do I need to marry? *Who* do I have to marry? How long do I have before I have to get married? It's some old weird man, isn't it?" I had to take a few deep breaths and try calm down. Aurora just looked at me with a smile and waved me over to sit next to her on the bed.

"I cannot tell you what you want to know, Ryan. All I can say is that I know your heart belongs to one another, even if you don't want to admit it to yourself. The man you must marry has a lot of trust to build back with you, but he is the one you need. He may not be the one you want right now, but he will be everything you have ever wanted, if you just give him a chance." God this is so frustrating. I hated not knowing who "he" was. A knock sounded at the door before I could ask Aurora anymore questions.

"Come in," I shouted, and Kai walked through the door a second later. The look on his beautiful face had me immediately jumping off the bed to stand in front of him. "What's wrong—why do you look so sad?"

"Because the time has come for me to leave you. I need to go back to Randall and explain why I helped you. I need to cover my tracks, he needs to think I was doing it so I would gain your trust. I'm sorry mi amor but I must make out like you mean nothing to me." I forgot all about Kai needing to leave; I didn't want him to go, if making out like he didn't care about me save his life, I was okay with that.

"I don't think it is safe for you to go back there, Kai. He could hurt you"

"The only person that could hurt me is you, mi amor. Don't worry, I will be fine, but I will probably be gone for a few days, so don't worry if I don't come back straight away. The others will watch over you and keep you safe." I didn't want to say goodbye to Kai, and the words I wanted to say wouldn't come out, so instead I let my actions speak for me. I leaned up on my tip-toes and pulled Kai's face down to mine and kissed him.

He was stiff as a board for a second, as I think I caught him off-guard, but then he snapped, grabbing me by the waist and pulling me flush against his chest, and I couldn't stop the moan that slipped free. Our tongues were intertwined and fighting for dominance. I needed more of him, and I went to put my hand under his shirt when a throat cleared and broke the spell that I was under. Kai reluctantly pulled back. That kiss was amazing. I looked over my shoulder to see where the noise came from, only to remember Aurora was still in the room. Oh my God, how embarrassing. I knew I was blushing, I could feel the heat in my cheeks.

"Well, I don't mean to interrupt, but I feel like a bit of a third wheel here." Kai and I both started laughing at Aurora's admission. I don't know what came over me. I'm a shy person— except for in my dreams, of course—and just with that thought I started blushing even harder.

"I must go now, mi amor, but stay safe. I shouldn't be gone long. If by any chance I don't return, you must carry on with your training and defeat Randall. You must promise me this." I could hear what he was saying, but I didn't want to think of the possibility that Kai might not come back. "Promise me, Ryan. I can see the fear in your eyes. I don't want you to be scared for me; I will be fine." I looked deep into his eyes and could see the desire he had for me, but I could also see that he meant every word; he wasn't scared for himself, and just knowing that gave me the strength to answer.

"I promise I will carry on training, but if you don't come back, just know that I will find a way to get you back and I'll burn Randall's fucking mansion down to get to you if I have to." With that said, I embraced Kai once more and held onto him like my life depended on it. I reluctantly let him go after a minute and watched him walk out the door. I felt like a part of my heart was leaving with him, and I had a feeling of dread in the pit of stomach, like something was going to go horribly wrong. I needed Kai to return so I could tell him that I loved him. That I had always loved him.

Chapter Twenty-Eight

Aurora and I made our way back to Jax's office to meet with the others and hopefully be able to talk to Nico. I needed the answers he held like I needed my next breath. I had to know why he kept this from me. Nico hiding this from me hurt, I trusted Nico. I confided in him and Kai in my dreams- never thinking they were real. They knew so much about me and I knew virtually nothing about them. I was more upset with the fact that I had such strong feelings for them both, what the hell was I going to do?

Once we were all inside and seated on the couches in Jax's office, I watched Dom in awe. He had these crystals that he was placing in a circle. Once they were arranged to his satisfaction, he went into the center of it and sat down with his legs crossed and head bent down, he began speaking in some foreign language.

"Portaly openinga feylinga realmy!" Once those words left his mouth, yellow sparks began flying from his outstretched hands, and then within a minute, Nico was standing in front of Dom. Dom quickly stood and gave Nico one of those man hugs.

Nico looked around the room, taking us all in, and then asked Dom.

"Why am I here brother?" I didn't let Dom answer, I was too pissed and wanted to get this show on the road.

"Because I need answers from you, and I want to know why the so-called king fucking lied to me." The sharp intake of breath from the others could be heard but I didn't pay them any attention. Nico and I were in a staring match.

"What answers are you wanting, love? And I also don't believe I have lied to you." Smug prick...I swear I never wanted to hit anyone so much in my life.

"I want to know why you helped my father lock away my powers, and why you fucking lied to me about knowing my father." His expression was unreadable.

"I never lied to you, love. You never asked me directly. We fae cannot lie; we may skirt around the truth, but if you ask us outright, we cannot lie."

"So answer my fucking question then! Why did you not tell me you knew my father?" I didn't realize I was crying until Nico walked over to me and wiped a tear from my cheek.

"I told you when I came to you in the cabin, as Simon that I knew your father." Nico looked around the room at the others, and then said. "Perhaps you might want to have this conversation in private, love. I don't believe it will be pleasant for you."

"We are not going anywhere, Stone." Trust Jax to be the first to speak; at least he wasn't growling this time.

"I want to stay; watching Ryan get pissed is so hot." Dom really needed to learn to filter his mouth. I could hear Tyler chuckling at Dom's comment, but I chose to ignore it. Nico was standing so still you would swear he was actually made of *stone*.

"I just want answers, Nico. Please, I need to know why you kept this from me." I couldn't keep the hurt out of my voice; I felt so betrayed by Nico once more. A look of anguish crossed his face before he quickly masked it.

"Fine, you might want to sit down, then, because it's a long story." if you wish for the others to stay then fine, but you all will remain quiet" Nico looked to everyone and gave them all a look that dared them to try defy him, no one did they all nodded and sat down, Nico and I both followed. I sat in the middle of Alex and Chase while Nico sat between Jax and Dom, Aurora sat on the single high back chair and Tyler stood behind her like a protector. Nico looked me right in the eyes before sighing; I had a feeling I wasn't going to like how this story went.

"When you were younger, your father sought me out. I do not know how he came to find me or how he even knew who I was. I lived in a different realm, after all, but I did come here every so often to keep an eye on Jax and Kai, even though we did not speak. I needed to know they were okay."

I felt a sense of respect for Nico in that moment; he didn't need to come and check on them, but he did it anyway. "One visit back here, I came alone without Dom for the first time. I decided to stop at the pub that we all used to go to and have a beer, for old times' sake. Once I was seated at the bar, a man came up to me and said, 'I've been waiting a long time for you.'"

"I had no idea who this brown-haired, green-eyed man was, but I knew he wasn't human. I automatically went on alert; I thought he was there to ambush me. Before I could attack him, he raised his hands and said, "I'm not here to hurt you, son. I'm here to ask for your help. You may not know me, but I know who you are, your majesty, and I believe that I can help you get your sister back if you just listen to me.

"I was shocked, but then anger overtook me. I didn't know how this man knew who I was or how he knew my sister was taken. I did the only thing I could think of—I told him to follow me outside, which he did. Once we were out front and around the corner where no one could see, I grabbed him by the throat and slammed him against the wall. I'm sorry, Ryan, but I was going to kill your father." I gasped; I couldn't believe Nico openly admitted he was going to hurt my dad, but before I could yell or scream at him, he continued. "He raised his hand at me and sent a blast of magic so strong it knocked me back several feet. I was going to charge him again, but he raised his hands in surrender and said, "I told you I'm not going to hurt you and I meant it. I'm here to ask for your help. Please—my daughter is in danger, and I don't know who else I can turn to."

"'Who the hell are you?' I asked him. 'I am Ralph Knox, head warlock to the Knox coven. You are Nicholas Stone, king of the fae. I mean you no harm, your majesty. I just need your help please, I believe my daughter is the key to eternal power, and she has the blood to seal the fae realm from Earth.'" My dad knew I was the key, he spent his life trying to help me. I would forever live with regret if not saying goodbye to my father.

"I didn't believe him at first, but the look on his face showed me he was genuinely scared for his child. I wanted to walk away and not help him, even if he was telling the truth that his daughter was the key to kill my people. Then I thought of Dom, Jax, and Kai, how we could be friends and trust each other, even though we were from different clans. Maybe this man could be trusted too. I agreed to meet with your father at a later time, as I had to get back to my realm. A week later I met your father at the same pub, but this time was different. I was keen to hear what he had to say, as I had done some research on what all the elders believed to be the key to power, and low and behold he was telling the truth—the blood of a witch-fae halfling with a pure heart is the key to seal the fae realm from Earth. Ralph and I spoke for hours about you, Ryan. God, he loved you so much he was willing to risk his life to find me just so you could live." I couldn't stay quiet anymore; I had to know.

"Why did my dad find you, though, and not someone else?" Nico gave me a sad smile, and I knew I wasn't going to like his answer.

"Because I am the only one strong enough to remove any fae's powers." My mouth dropped open at that. I mean, what the actual fuck? Dom scoffed, clearly not impressed that Nico said his magic was the strongest.

"So you knew when you sent us back here that I could never learn how to control my powers, because I didn't even have all of them!"

"It's not that simple, love. Let me finish the story and you will understand why I did what I did, okay?" I gave him a curt nod to continue. "I told your father that before I was willing to strip someone—even a child—of their gifts, I needed to see for myself that this child did in fact have both witch and fae powers. I was there that day when your father took you to the park. You never saw me, but I was there." Creepy, but okay. "I watched you and saw that you had no evil whatsoever in your body. I just saw light, and I was awestruck by your gentle and forgiving nature. You were abused so terribly by your mother, but you never let the darkness consume you.

"You are strong, Ryan. Do not ever forget that your strength grows within you every day. All I did was put a block on your powers—I never stripped them. I couldn't strip them, if I'm being totally honest."

"Why couldn't you strip them?" Alex asked.

"Because she is too powerful. She possesses even more power than me and Dom." Holy shit balls! I could tell by the look in Nico's eyes that he was telling the truth—he really thought I was that powerful. "Also I didn't even want to try, because there was a chance you might die, and I wasn't willing to take that risk."

"Why did you do it, though? I don't understand why you

would help my dad when you just said you didn't trust him. Why not just kill me?" Nico started looking around the room, almost like he didn't want the others to hear the answer to my question.

"Because I felt a connection to you that I can't explain. I know that doesn't make much sense to you, love, but I just knew one day our paths would cross again, and you would need my help. So I did the only thing I could think of, which was to block your powers, so when the day came that you would need to access them, you would have to come find me. I could never hurt you, Ryan." I don't know why, but his admission had me swooning a bit, in spite of the fact that the look in his eyes told me there was more to this story. Nico was still hiding something from me, and I wanted to know what it was.

"Now that you're done eye fucking my cousin *your majesty,* can we get back on track here" I couldn't help but blush at Chases' statement, everyone in the room just saw me melting all over the Fae King. To break the awkwardness I cleared my throat and asked.

"What happens now then?"

"That's the tricky part, love; unlocking your powers is going to be painful."

"Why would it hurt her?" Bless you, Jax, for asking the question I was too scared to say out loud.

"What I mean is that when I unlock the other half of Ryan's powers, it will be like letting a caged animal run free for the first time. Her powers have been locked up since before she hit puberty, so it will burn through her, so to speak. We will have to manage it as best we can and try to help her control it, or she could seriously hurt someone or even herself." I was sucking in huge amounts of air—I mean, it sounds like I was about to burn Jax's whole compound to the ground, and the last thing I wanted to do was hurt anyone. "Well, it'll be best to do this outside, where no one is around, so maybe in the woods?" I don't know who Nico was directing his question to, but Dom was the one to answer him.

"We'll go to the woods, when everyone is at dinner, and I'll put a ward around us to try control the damage to the area."

"Why would we need a ward? You're making it sound like she's going to blow up!" Alex snapped.

"There is a chance that there could be a huge blast. Like I said, Ryan is very powerful, and with me unlocking this side of her powers that she has never had to deal with, it could cause her to lash out to stop the pain. She won't know how to control all the power coursing through her veins." Well, Nico was shit at pep talks, wasn't he?

"I will be there to help guide and train her to harness the energy," Aurora chimed in. I was glad that no one had mentioned me getting married. I was really hoping that they had forgotten that bit; I didn't want to marry anyone. I was too young for that, Nico never said I had to marry in order for him to release my powers. I was counting that as a win.

I tuned everyone out while they made plans for what was to happen this evening, I couldn't take the pressure, so I walked out of the room and headed back to my temporary bedroom, somewhat amazed I found my way back there. Once inside, I plopped down on the bed and covered my eyes with my arm. I just needed to be alone and to think. But that wasn't apparently an option, because almost as soon as I had the thought, there was a knock on my door.

"WHAT?" I bellowed.

"Do you mind if we come in?" At the sound of Jax's voice, I quickly sat up. It wasn't just Jax, though—he was followed in by Dom and Nico. They all stood awkwardly at the end of my bed, but given that I'd left them for peace and quiet, and they're the ones who came to my room, I wasn't going to be the one to talk first.

"I know this is a lot for you to take in, but we're trying to help and make this as easy as possible for you," said Dom.

"I know you guys are, it's just hard to process the amount of mind-boggling information I'm getting hit with. I don't want to hurt anyone and I sure as shit don't want to hurt myself."*Or get married.*

"We're not asking you to hurt anyone, love— were just asking that you let Dom and Aurora train you to allow you to get some sort of control over your powers, so when the time comes, maybe the reality that your enemies know you know how to harm them will scare them enough to back down." I wish what Jackson was arguing could happen, but we all knew that Randall Cane wouldn't back down without a fight.

"Okay, I'll agree to Dom and Aurora training me, but you all have to promise me that no matter what happens, none of you will harm my sister." They all exchanged looks with one another and agreed. "I've also been wondering—Randall drank from me at the cabin. I guess that means he's going to be strong and powerful now, right?"

"No, Randall will be the same strength as he normally is. Your fae side isn't unlocked yet, so he only drank your witch blood, so to speak." Nico's answer made me feel slightly less fucked, which was a pleasant surprise.

"We must begin the training as soon as we can. I have a feeling Randall won't sit by much longer; he's chronically impatient, so something must be wrong if he is not attacking us already." Dom sounded so sure, which made me worry even more for Kai. What if something happened to him? What if they knew he was helping us? Would they harm him?

"Do you think if Randall found out Kai was helping us, that he would kill him?" They all shared an ominous look, which gave me the answer to my question. "By the looks on your faces, I'm assuming that's a big fat yes." Dread filled my stomach. I couldn't explain it, but I just knew Kai was in trouble and needed our help—I could feel it in my soul.

"Look, Kai is strong, and he is a great solider. The best there is, really. Randall has known for a while that Kai hasn't been himself. Kai is loyal to a fault, and if Randall has sensed that his loyalties are shifting, he will try to take him out." Nico wasn't sugar-coating the truth.

"I can't explain it, but I have the worst feeling that Kai is in trouble and needs our help. I feel like he's trying to tell me something, but I don't' know what. I felt this pulling sensation, like I do in my dreams but nothing is happening. Could that be Kai?" Dom's face went from calm to serious in half a second.

"Ryan, sweetheart, I need you to lie down, okay? The only way Kai can come to you from a distance and without touch is if you are asleep." I did as Dom asked without question and shuffled up to the top of the bed. "Okay, I'm going to do a sleeping spell, love, which will take you to Kai and—"

"I'm going under with her, in case it's a trap." Nico was looking me straight in the eye, and I knew by the look on his face that he wasn't going to take no for an answer, so I just nodded. He climbed on the other side of the bed, linking his fingers through mine, and I felt like a zap of electricity had shot through my arm just from that small contact. I always felt a spark when Nico touched me.

"Okay, well, I guess I'll be putting you both under then, Jax, and I will stand watch to make sure you're both fine. If anything happens, pull her out straight away, Nico." Nico gave Dom a firm nod and closed his eyes, I leaned back and closed my eyes as well and listened to Dom chanting in another language. I didn't feel anything happening for a while, and then all of a sudden everything went dark.

Chapter Twenty-Nine

Being here at the lake with Nico felt wrong; this was my and Kai's place—well, one of them. We would meet in the forest or at this lake. It was beautiful, with serene water that mirrored the surrounding forest and mountains. The silence here is what made this my favorite place on Earth.

Never have both men been in my dream at the same time. I knew I loved Kai; I've always known that, at least subconsciously. The more I am around Nico, the more I'm starting to feel things for him. I love Kai, but I love Nico too. My heart needs to stay out of this. I have no right falling for either of them. Shaking myself out of my thoughts, I call out for him.

"Kai?"

He always came when I called. This time it felt different, like something was off. I can't explain it but, I just felt it. I heard a branch break, only to find Nico, not Kai, which was slightly worrying.

"Where is he?"

"I don't know. He's always here, Nico—he never makes me wait."

Nico came over and wrapped an arm around my shoulders.

I appreciated the gesture; I didn't feel so alone in his embrace. I was thankful to have him here with me, now. I was scared for Kai, I just knew something was wrong, I could feel it.

"Kai, please come out! Nico and I are here."

My bad feeling about Kai was getting worse. I felt cold, and I never felt uncomfortable in my dreams. I always felt warm, like in springtime. I heard some branches snapping and quickly spun toward the noise. Nico and I both gasped at the sight, my heart sank.

Kai limped towards us, only to stumble, and grab a tree trunk before he could fall to the ground. Nico rushed over and caught him, then eased him down carefully on the ground by the side of the lake. I rushed over and knelt down beside him. His face was covered in blood, with black bruises marring his beautiful face. He only wore a pair of shorts, and his legs were covered in wounds. I noticed his fingers and toes had no nails.

"Oh my God, they're torturing you, aren't they?" I started to cry. Kai was in so much pain, and I could tell he was trying to mask it for my benefit. He tried to lift his hand to wipe away my tears, but he didn't have the strength to even do that. He turned away from me and looked to Nico.

"I have fulfilled my vow to you, my brother. Your sister is free and making her way to Jackson's camp as we speak." Nico jerked back, obviously shocked by the revelation. "You must warn Jackson that his second in command is a traitor. Randall knew I was coming and that I was helping Ryan."

"How?" Nico snapped.

"Tyler and Stevie are working together, and he has been feeding her information." Kai turned toward me then. "You must not come for me, mi amor, no matter what. " I started to protest, but Kai cut me off. "It is a trap. Randall knows you will come for me, and by the time you get to me, I will already be dead." I started sobbing in earnest now, holding onto his face and smoothing back his hair. "I don't have long left—I can feel my life force fading now."

"Don't cry, mi amor, I am grateful I got to have any time with you at all. I need you to listen to me now." I nodded so he could continue.

"Your sister is not coming back from this, Ryan" I started to shake my head; I had to believe I could save Stevie. "She is the one torturing me with Randall, and she enjoys it so much more because she knows that hurting me will hurt you." Rage like I had never known surged within me. How could she do this to Kai? I could hear Kai's breathing start to shorten, and I knew deep down he was dying.

"Nico, please you have to help him, I am begging you, please!" Tears were streaming down my face. I couldn't lose Kai. Nico looked sick with grief. "Why the hell aren't you helping him, Nico? He's your fucking friend! Cast a fucking spell or something!" I shouted. He just looked at me with tears in his eyes.

"I can't heal the dead, Ryan. There is nothing I can do." I wanted to argue with him, but I could see he was just as angry and heartbroken as I was. I tore my gaze away from Nico and looked down at my strong and courageous vampire. I couldn't stop the tears falling.

"Do not cry for me *mi amor*, I will see you again" he sounded so certain, almost like a promise.

"I love you, Melakai. I always wished you were real. And when I finally got my wish granted, I wasted so much time. I am so sorry, Kai. I swear on all that is holy in this world that I will avenge you and make anyone who hurt you suffer. You have my word." I leaned down and kissed his cold, chapped lips. And then it all went black.

I awoke next to Nico on the bed. Before anyone could say anything, Nico grabbed me and pulled me into his embrace. I started crying—great heaving sobs. The dream ended because Kai was gone. She fucking killed him.

"I am so sorry, we couldn't save him," Nico stuttered out.

"Wait, what the hell do you mean? You couldn't save who, Nico? Where the fuck is Kai?" Dom was shouting at Nico, I could hear in his voice he knew the answer to his own question, but he didn't want to believe it.

Nico had to answer for us. "We couldn't save Melakai. They killed him."

I drew in a steadying breath. I could feel the lump in my throat and had to push past it. "We need to unlock my powers and I need to train. We are going to war, and we are going to kill every single one of those fucking sons of bitches, and my sister is at the top of the list."

Epilogue

NICO

I held her sobbing form for over an hour. I understand her heart is broken for the loss of my brother, whom she thinks she loves. She has no idea what she wants, but I will be the one to show and guide her through all this. Now she is finally sleeping, her beautiful long brown hair fanned out behind her. Jackson and Dom haven't left the room. They each sit in the single high back chairs, their eyes glued to my girl. Their grief clear on their faces, they are hurt by the loss of Kai. We all are, we just lost our brother.

"Jackson, I need a favor." Jackson reluctantly pulls his stare from Ryan.

"What do you need, Nico?"

"I need some of your men to find my sister. Kai set her free." I can hear both Jackson and Dominic's sharp intake of air. Neither of them expected those words to come from my mouth, especially not after learning of Kai's death. I don't know how Kai knew where she was or how he even set her free, I owed Melakai a debut. He fulfilled the vow he made to me seventeen years ago.

"You have my word. I'll go myself and make sure she is okay."

"Jax, I'll go with you," Dom said. I thanked both my brothers as they exited the room and shut the door. Now I finally have a moment alone with my girl.

"When you wake, I will tell you everything, my love. You are so much more than you even know." I move my free hand to my back pocket and feel the outline of the envelope. I stole the letter her dad wrote her. I never opened or read it, but I couldn't leave it there when I snuck into her room to see her. I am no thief, but I also didn't want her bitch of a sister getting her grubby hands on it. This letter may contain information that we can't afford Stevie to have. Before I can continue my train of thought, the door opens and Aurora walks in.

"Have you told her, Nico?"

"No, I will tell her when the time is right."

"You need to tell her immediately. She deserves to know the truth."

"Her heart is broken right now, and if I drop this bomb on her, she will hate me more than she already does."

"Stop being so selfish, she has a right to know!"

"That is not your fucking secret to tell!" I'm shouting now; I need to calm down and keep quiet or risk waking Ryan.

"Tell her the truth, and do it soon, or I will, Nico."

"I'll tell her as soon as you tell Jax that she isn't really his *mate*." I hear her gasp, and her pale blue eyes turn stormy.

"I'll tell Jackson the truth as soon as you tell Ryan you are her future husband. You can also tell her the truth about where her mother really is, while you're at it. I'm sure she would love to know how *close* she is to her abuser."

I am so fucking screwed.

Click the link to download book 2,

Fate

Also by Samantha Barrett

Mafia Romance

<u>Murdoch Mafia Series</u>

Played By The Bishop

Tormented By The King

Tortured By The Knight

Tempted By The Queen

Turned By The Pawn

Ruined By The Rook

<u>Murdoch Mafia Novella</u>

Stalemate

<u>Memento Mori Series</u>

Reign Of Royal

Broken By Sin

In Havoc Lays Chaos

<u>Godfathers of the night</u>

London has Fallen

Damned By His Angel

<u>Re Della Strada</u>

Shattered Soul

Fractured Heart

Tainted Essence

<u>Fairytales With A Twist</u>

Condemned Beast

Secret Society/ Bully

Filthy Few

Forever Filthy

Filthiest Of Them All

Masked Men Novella (Pure Smut)

Dirty Priest

Dirty Daddy

Sports Romance

<u>Playing For Keeps</u>

Offside

Touchdown

End Game

Hail Mary

Blindside

RH Sports

Hate Us Like You Mean It

MM

Love Me Like You Mean It

Paranormal Romance

<u>The Veil Of Obsidian</u>

Of Time And Carnage

<u>Curse Of Fate</u>

Dream

Fate

Nightmare

Redemption

Anarchy

<u>Brutal Savages</u>

Savage Lies

Brutal Truth

Savage Beast

Brutal Beauty

Acknowledgments

I would like to thank my husband for his patience, understanding and love while I was writing. You are my inspiration and my muse for this book, thank you for pushing me to chase my dreams.

Thank you to my beautiful children for being you and inspiring me every day.

Thank you to my Mum and my Step-Dad for being there for me and believing in me. Without you both, '*A Beautiful Dream*' wouldn't have been published.

Thank you to my Dad for always teaching me to never settle and to always aim higher.

Special shout out to Kelsey Clayton, for helping me and helping me navigate my way through self-publishing, you truly are amazing.

About the Author

Samantha Barrett is originally from Auckland, New Zealand but living in Brisbane, Australia.

Sam writes all things dirty dark and delicious with a side of twisted mind fuck.

She is a lover of all things red flags and an anti-hero is a must.

www.ingramcontent.com/pod-product-compliance
Lightning Source LLC
Chambersburg PA
CBHW030425120726
47903CB00003B/813